Never had any...
this....

Chas's world tilted. ...
as her gaze darted a... ...many she forced her
frozen voice to speak. "I don't know what to say."

"You don't have to say anything. I just wanted to tell you."

He was smiling and relaxed.

She couldn't look directly at him.

One blaring question resounded in her brain. What did his confession mean?

She hurried toward the door, mumbling something about how much she'd enjoyed seeing his work, and stumbled outside. Emma would be wondering what was taking her so long, but Chas needed time to think, to let her tumbled thoughts settle. Her steps took her down the residential street, past the big turreted houses toward the white picket fence. As she passed, her eyes sought the arbor enclosing the table and chairs.

She choked back a sob. Her own father, Simon LaBlanc, had not cared enough to find out who she was. Yet a man she remembered only as a boy in school had carried her picture for ten years. *In his heart.*

She had told Adam she'd been raised to know she was special—a gift from God. But never had anything made her feel as special as this.

LINDA FORD draws on her own experiences living in the Canadian prairie and Rockies to paint wonderful adventures in romance and faith. She lives in Alberta, Canada, with her family, writing as much as her full-time job of taking care of a paraplegic and four kids who are still at home will allow. Linda says, "I thank God that He has given me a full, productive life and that I'm not bored. I thank Him for placing a little bit of the creative energy revealed in His creation into me, and I pray I might use my writing for His honor and glory."

HEARTSONG PRESENTS

Books by Linda Ford
HP240—The Sun Still Shines
HP268—Unchained Hearts
HP368—The Heart Seeks a Home

Chastity's Angel

Linda Ford

Heartsong Presents

For Carolyne Aarsen: friend and fellow writer. Thank you for your patient listening, your encouragement, and help. Perhaps beneath that wide smile and zany laugh is an angel.

A note from the author:
I love to hear from my readers! You may correspond with me by writing:

Linda Ford
Author Relations
PO Box 719
Uhrichsville, OH 44683

ISBN 1-58660-321-3

CHASTITY'S ANGEL

All Scripture quotations, unless otherwise noted, are taken from the King James Version of the Bible.

All of the characters and events in this book are fictitious. Any resemblance to actual persons, living or dead, or to actual events is purely coincidental.

Cover design by Jocelyne Bouchard.

PRINTED IN THE U.S.A.

one

Everything seemed to happen at once that pleasant summer afternoon of 1909 at Brownlee's Boardinghouse in the thriving town of Willow Creek, Alberta, Canada.

Chastity stood in the kitchen, her nimble fingers rolling out dough, fitting it into the pie dishes, and laying aside perfect circles for the top crust. She breathed in the heady scent of the last lilacs of the season and listened to the cheery call of the robin in the backyard. Occasionally she glanced out the open window to drink in the brightness of the cornflower blue sky and the fullness of green in the row of poplar trees marching down the side of the yard.

As her hands worked, Chastity's thoughts flitted from one subject to another with no more concern than a butterfly tasting of the bounty of flowers in a summer meadow.

For a moment she thought of supper. The roast was in the oven; she had plenty of time to peel vegetables and finish the pies. A smile tugged at her lips as she anticipated the boarders' eager reaction to hot rhubarb pie. Then she remembered a conversation she'd had earlier with Emma, the hired girl, about mending the sheets from Mrs. Banner's room. From there her thoughts had drifted to planning tea, then to Michael and how he—

Just then the back doorbell clanged. It would be her grocery order.

At the same time she heard a crash from the dining room, where she had left her mother polishing the silver teapot.

"Come in!" she called to the back door and in the next breath to the dining room, "Mother?" And before she could gasp in more air, she cried out, "Emma!" She only hoped that Emma, out in the garden pulling rhubarb, would hear her.

5

The back door squeaked, but Chas didn't even glance at the delivery boy. Her throat constricting, she dashed for the dining room.

Her mother lay in a heap on top of the statue that ordinarily stood beside her chair. The teapot quivered against the table leg.

"Mother, what happened?"

Her mother groaned and tried to disentangle herself from the statue and chair legs.

"Wait, Mother—I'll help." She bent down to the stricken woman.

Footsteps thudded in the doorway, and, without turning, the young woman called over her shoulder to the delivery boy, "Could you give me a hand, please?"

The boy stepped to her side. It flashed through her mind that the hands were awfully large for the boy Mr. Silverhorn usually sent, but glad for strong arms to lift her mother, she gave it no more thought.

Still on her knees, she ran her hands along her mother's legs.

"I'm all right, *Cherie.*"

Chas looked into her mother's face and, seeing her pallor, found no reassurance in the words.

"What happened?" Chas narrowed her eyes. She'd left her mother strict instructions to call if she needed anything, but the polish and rag were on the table, too far to reach without leaving the chair. "What were you up to?"

Her mother sighed. "I only wanted to put the teapot on the sideboard." She leaned back. "My leg went out from under me."

Emma skidded through the doorway. "What on earth's going on? The door's wide open, and the groceries are spilled all over the table." She gulped. "Miz LaBlanc, what happened? You look as if you've seen a ghost." Before anyone could respond, Emma answered her own question. "Ah, I think you've been naughty again."

Chas stood to her feet. "Emma, run and get Doc Johnson, please."

The mother waved her hand. "No, no, that isn't necessary." She moaned. "Chastity, please get one of those tablets he left."

Chas hesitated. As much as the sight of her mother in pain frightened her, a tremor of anger passed through her. How could she so blithely ignore the doctor's warnings to let her hip heal before trying to use it?

The woman shifted and flinched.

Chas turned and hurried down the hall toward their private suite. The pill bottle stood on her mother's bedside table. She shook a tablet into her palm and hurried back, pausing in the kitchen long enough to fill a glass with water. "Here, take this."

"*Merci,* my dear." The woman tipped her head back and swallowed, closing her eyes and resting her head on the back of the burgundy wing chair.

Slowly she opened her eyes, focusing them on something to the right of her daughter.

Chas turned to follow the direction of her mother's gaze and saw the delivery boy standing a few feet away. She swallowed a gasp. This was no boy. He had a thick mop of blond hair dipping over one eye. Dark blue eyes returned her stare. Chas's cheeks grew hot, but she couldn't stop staring.

"Why, it's Adam, isn't it?" Her mother's voice shattered her trance, and Chas pulled her gaze away. "Adam Silverhorn."

"Yes, Ma'am."

"So you finally decided to return."

"Yes, Ma'am." He grinned at her.

"About time, I'd say."

"Yes, Ma'am." He chuckled. "I kind of thought so myself."

Chas studied him openly. The last time she'd seen him, he was a scrawny youth with a habit of plunging into trouble. Then he had up and disappeared, following the gold rush to the Klondike, or so the story went. She tried to think if she had heard where he'd been since then.

"So where have you been all this time?" her mother prodded.

Again Adam chuckled. "How long do you have?"

"Why don't you take tea with us and tell me?"

Chas jumped to attention. She had forgotten tea.

Behind her, Emma groaned. "The dearies will be here expecting everything to be ready." She hastened to the door. "I'll put the kettle on."

"I'd better hurry," Chas muttered and, turning to leave, stubbed her toe on the statue. She leaned over to set it upright.

"Let me." Adam bent over at the same time. Their faces were so close she could see the glittering streaks in his irises.

She let him straighten the heavy statue. Suddenly she began to laugh. Adam regarded her with raised eyebrows. Out of the corner of her eye, she saw her mother's startled expression.

"Did I miss something?" Adam asked, looking at her.

Chas pointed at the statue. "It's Mother's protecting angel." Made of rough white pottery, the statue was an angel with wings folded at his back, a sword resting on the ground at his feet. She grinned. "Perhaps he was sleeping," she said to her mother.

"Away with you. You couldn't blame an angel for an old woman's foolishness."

Adam smiled at the woman. "Now, Miz LaBlanc, you don't look a day older than when I last saw you ten years ago."

Mother narrowed her eyes. "And I'm thinking you've developed a silver tongue to go with that last name of yours."

Chas headed toward the kitchen, scooping the teapot off the floor as she left.

Emma, busy placing china teacups on the big tray, turned as Chas hurried into the kitchen. "So that's Adam Silverhorn." She pressed her palm against her chest. "Be still, my racing heart." Fixing her eyes on Chas, she demanded, "Why didn't you tell me he was so dreamy looking?"

Instead of answering right away, Chas washed the teapot and warmed it with hot water. "Put some cookies on the flowered china serving plate." She scooped a handful of tea leaves into the warmed pot and filled it with boiling water. "I remember him with a nose that seemed too large for his face and arms too long for his sleeves." Her cheeks warmed again as she thought how she had stared unmercifully at the poor man. "He seems to have outgrown all that." She nodded. "I expect he'll set your poor young heart all aflutter."

Emma sniffed. "Oh, you old grandma. I declare. I don't know how you manage without your cane." Her voice wheezed and wobbled. Then she glared at Chas. "I am eighteen, you know. You make six years sound like a lifetime."

Chas sighed as she arranged the serving tray. "It feels like it sometimes."

Beyond the far door, hinges creaked, and a shuffling sound started down the hall.

"Hurry. Take in the serving tray." Chas grabbed the teapot and followed Emma's heels to the sitting room. They set up tea on the small table reserved for this ritual. "You look after things while I get Mother." She hurried across the hall to the dining room, pausing in the doorway to take in the scene.

Adam had pulled a chair close to her mother's side and, leaning back, spoke to the older woman.

"It was like nothing you could imagine. In fact, if I didn't have the photos and drawings to prove it, many people would call me a liar."

His voice was low and lazy yet filled with a melody that told Chas whatever he was talking about gave him pleasure and excitement.

Mother turned and saw her daughter. "It's teatime, Adam. Do join us. You can tell me more." She nodded toward Chas. "Get my cane—will you, Dear? I think I left it in the hall."

Chas retrieved it from outside the door. "I can't imagine what Doc Johnson is going to say when you have to explain you decided you could get along without this."

Her mother leaned forward, one hand on top of her cane. "Never you mind, young lady. I'm not going to cry over spilt milk. What's done is done. I'll just be more careful from now on." She reached a hand for Adam's arm. "If you'd be so good as to assist me to the other room—"

"My pleasure."

Chas grinned. Her mother had a way of bringing out the best and the kindest in people.

Following them to the sitting room, she glanced around. Mrs. Banner had eased into the armless padded chair where she always sat and peered over her glasses as the trio entered the room. Her head bobbed up and down as she watched the procession.

"Marie." She focused on Mother, then tilted her nose to study Adam. "Who is this young man?"

Mother lowered herself into the rocking chair across from Mrs. Banner, murmuring her thanks to Adam and waving him to the chair at her side.

"Ida," she leaned toward the older woman and raised her voice, "you remember Adam. Adam Silverhorn."

Mrs. Banner drew back in the chair. "Pshaw. Why would I want corn? This is teatime," she said with a huff.

"No, no." Mother's voice grew louder. "Not corn. Silverhorn."

Mrs. Banner pulled her handkerchief through her fingers. "I don't care if it is summer corn. All I want are tea and cookies." She looked down her nose at the other woman. "Now who is this young man?"

Chas turned away, hiding a smile. Sometimes there was simply no way of getting through to Mrs. B, but Mother never seemed ruffled from trying.

"Adam. Adam from the store."

Mrs. B bobbed her head, several gray hairs straying around her face. "Why didn't you say so? Now where's that girl with the tea?"

Emma set the cup at her elbow.

Even though Chas knew exactly what Mrs. B would want, she played out the ritual, carrying the creamer and sugar bowl to the regal lady. "Would you like milk or sugar?"

"I do believe I'll have a little of each. A rounded spoonful of sugar and a splash of milk, if you please."

Chas knew without looking that Emma would be silently

mouthing the words, and she lowered her head to avoid the girl's knowing wink.

"Adam, would you like tea?"

His eyes flashed with bright spears of silver. For a moment his look seemed to isolate the two of them.

Emma shoved the plate of cookies under his elbow. "Cookies, Adam?"

Chas turned away, setting the creamer and sugar bowl on the tea table.

The clock on the mantle bonged three times. Chas straightened, listening, and met Emma's eyes. Upstairs a door closed with a muted thud, and footsteps could be heard crossing the length of the hall and descending the stairs.

Emma waggled her eyebrows. "You could set your clock by him."

A stiffly upright man stepped through the door, his gait measured and precise.

"Good afternoon, Mr. Elias," Mother murmured. "Tea is ready."

"Good afternoon."

His nod included them all. He took the cup Emma offered and sat ramrod straight on a hard wooden chair, the light from the window glistening on his head.

Chas sat on the overstuffed green sofa and glanced around. This was her home—the only home she had ever known and certainly a home like no other. But despite its unusual nature, she had been surrounded by love here. Every aspect of her life had been overshadowed by the knowledge of God's love. She turned and met her mother's gaze and smiled.

This ritual was almost as old as she was. Afternoon tea—punctually at two fifty-five. Over the years some of the regulars had gone, while others had come to take their place—some for a short time; others, like Mr. Elias, for longer periods. Mrs. B had been there longer than Chas or even her mother.

They each had their special chair—not by right of ownership but by silent consent. Teacups were arranged in their own fashion—her mother's on the stool at her knee; Mrs. B's at her elbow on the skirted round table; Mr. Elias's balanced in one hand.

The room itself was as unchangeable as the tea ritual. The same burgundy drapes were fastened back with the same faded wine-colored rope. Despite her subtle attempts, Chas had been unsuccessful in changing a single feature. Every knickknack was quickly returned to its original position as soon as she left the room, each chair shoved back to its precise placement. Even the angel picture hanging over the fireplace had remained unchanged since before her birth. She looked up at it. A kind-faced angel robed in a white gown caught the fingertips on the out-flung hand of a child stepping on rocks as she made her way across a swiftly flowing river.

Indeed, the only thing different was Adam's presence, and every eye sought him.

"Mr. Elias," Mother said, her voice soft and gentle, "this is Adam, Ed Silverhorn's son."

Mr. Elias nodded his head in acknowledgment. "Pleased to meet you."

"He was telling me about his trip to the Klondike." She tilted her head to Adam. "And where else did you say?"

Adam stood and shook Mr. Elias's hand, returning to his seat before he answered. "I spent three years in the Klondike and two more in Alaska. From there I explored down the coastline and among the Gulf Islands. After that I spent some time in the interior of B.C." He shrugged. "Then I decided I was heading in the right direction and came home."

Chas let her breath out in a little whistle. "All that in ten years!" She shook her head. She had been no further than the edge of town. "Did you find gold?"

He chuckled. "No. Found something better, though."

She squinted at him. "Better than gold?"

"Yes," he said, nodding. "I found life."

She studied him. Life was what you made of it. Life was here and now. It was found in making wise choices and adjusting. It was in being content where God put you. There was no need to chase off to the ends of the world to find life and live it, and his suggestion of it made her want to argue.

Adam spoke before she could do more than open her mouth. "I can see you're wondering what I mean." He leaned back and smiled up at the ceiling as if seeing something wonderful and elusive. "I got to see firsthand the events that are making history. I recorded them. And for the most part I lived them." He suddenly lowered his head and fixed her with a sharp look. "That's what I mean."

She pulled her gaze away, studying the brown liquid in her cup. "Some of us live life in the minuscule, seeing it and experiencing it and enjoying it through the tiny details of every day." She straightened, and her gaze locked with his. "The beauty of the sunset, the sweetness of the lilac blossoms, the sound of the birds singing. We learn to take what God has given us and appreciate it."

Emma sighed. "But how exciting to be able to see so many new and wonderful things. It thrills me. Tell me, Mr. Silverhorn—what was the most wonderful thing you saw?"

"Please call me Adam." His expression grew serious. "I guess I would have to agree with Chastity. It's the wonders of nature that are the most profound."

His blue eyes forbade Chas to turn away when she would have dismissed his pronouncement. "When I saw the sun glistening off the great glaciers of the Yukon and realized the challenge the snow-covered mountains would be to the puny men trying to scale them—" He half laughed. "Well, I was so awestruck I could barely breathe."

Chas tried to pull her gaze away. She tried to blink. But she was caught by his intensity.

Emma let out a whoosh of air. "It sounds wonderful."

"Adam," Mother said, "you mentioned photos and drawings."

He turned toward her, and Chas sank back against the cushions. "Yes, I have quite a collection. I tried to record everything I saw."

She nodded. "Perhaps we can see some of your recordings."

"Of course." He relaxed. "I plan to display some of them at my shop, but I have hundreds more than I can display. I'd be glad to bring some for you to see." His glance included Chas.

She pressed her finger to her lips. Adam Silverhorn might have grown from a gangly youth to a handsome well-built man; he might have seen life, as he put it. But she wasn't about to let him turn her life upside down with talk of faraway places and exciting events. She knew the boundaries of her life, and right now they were the four walls of Brownlee's Boardinghouse. And with that she was content. There was only one thing she wished she could change—

"A shop?" her mother asked.

"I'm planning to turn the side room Father uses for storage into a photography shop. That way I can help in the store and continue with my own business as well."

Mr. Elias nodded. "It sounds to me as if you've had yourself a fine adventure, young fella." Without bending his back, he stood to his feet, setting his cup on the tea table. "Now if you will all excuse me, I must leave." And he marched from the room.

Chas did not have to listen to know his steps would lead up the stairs and into his room, where he would get his coat and then walk back down the stairs and out the front door. He would be gone exactly one hour and thirty minutes and return to his room until precisely fifteen minutes before the evening meal, when he would once again descend the stairs. The only variable was whether or not he would take a small parcel with him or return from his outing with one.

Emma's dark comments one time had sparked curiosity as to the contents of the parcels.

Mrs. B's fingers fussed at the variegated pink doily she had withdrawn from her cloth bag.

Chas caught the sorrow in her mother's look and swallowed back her own sadness. Mrs. B's joints were daily growing more stiff, and her eyes were no longer able to pick out the stitches as she crocheted. Chas was certain she worked as much by feel as by sight. The current project was knotted and curled.

Her mother reached out for the doily. "You've made good progress, Ida. This is lovely."

"I can't seem to get the pattern quite right," Mrs. B said, her voice thin. "Could you see what's the matter, Marie?"

Mother held the half-made doily in her lap and quickly pulled out several rows. "I think I can solve the problem." She took the hook from Mrs. B's lap, made a few stitches and gave the handiwork back to the older lady. "It was only a knot."

Mrs. B bent close, examining it as much with her fingers as her eyes. She sighed and lifted her head. "Thank you, Marie. I'm sorry to be such a bother."

Mother patted her hand. "Ida, you are never a bother."

Emma stood up. "I guess I'd better get back to work." She paused in front of Adam. "I think your life sounds real exciting. I wish I could do something like that." Then she laughed. "But since it's doubtful I'll ever get the chance, I'd love to see your pictures."

Adam stood to his feet and smiled at her. "That's what they're for—to give people who can't be there the chance to see what it was like."

Chas followed Emma. As she started to pass Adam, he murmured, "It's good to see you again."

She stopped and turned to meet his gaze. Ten years ago she was barely more than a child. She narrowed her eyes. What did he remember of her back then?

"Thank you for tea," he said with a grin, as if guessing her thoughts.

"You're welcome," she said and fled to the kitchen.

But if she thought the kitchen would provide relief from thinking about Adam, she had forgotten to take Emma into account.

The girl grabbed her arm and whispered, "Isn't he something? Almost too good to be true."

"Emma! Just because he's been to the Klondike and back

doesn't make him exceptional. Besides, what about his poor parents? I wonder how they felt about him disappearing into the wild blue yonder for so long?" She pursed her lips. "How old is Jack Silverhorn? Nine. Ten. Why, I'd venture a guess Jack was born after Adam left."

"And you'd be right." The deep voice behind her almost made her choke. "Furthermore, Ellen was only seven. That's part of the reason I've come back. I wanted to get to know my little brother and sister."

Chas swallowed hard and forced herself to turn toward him. "Forgive me," she murmured. "I have no right to concern myself with your affairs."

"It hasn't offended me," he said with a chuckle, his eyes shining.

"Matter of fact, I expect I'll be the center of a lot of speculation. And I expect I can handle it."

Emma stepped over to Adam, her face glowing. "I think it's wonderful you've come back. So will everyone else."

"More than likely most of them will think I'm crazy," he said, his gaze never leaving Chas's face. "Crazy for going, crazy for the work I do, and crazier still for coming home and bringing it with me. Isn't that right, Chas?"

At this Chas had to smile. She shook her head. "No, I don't think 'crazy' would be the word most people would use." She pressed her finger to her lips. "Let's see, maybe strange, unusual—" She blinked. Those were the same words she was sure people used to describe her life. "You're right. I think you'll be able to live with it."

He nodded and then turned toward the table. "I'm sorry I dumped your groceries like that." He picked up the sack of oatmeal. "Where do you want me to put this?"

Chas had been about to say he didn't need to bother, but Emma spoke up. "In the pantry—I'll show you."

Adam followed her. Chas turned to the pile of rhubarb Emma had flung on the table. It had to be washed, chopped, and hurried into the pies if they were to be baked in time.

After she and Adam returned, Emma picked up the basin of potatoes and grabbed a paring knife. Adam paused at the table, and Chas glanced up to see what he wanted.

"I'm sorry about your mother's accident. Will she be all right?"

Chas gulped. "I don't know if she'll ever be all right again."

"What do you mean?"

She looked down again, continuing her task as she talked. "She fell down the stairs almost two years ago. She was carrying an armload of washing and didn't realize how close she was to the first step." Chastity took a deep breath. "Doc Johnson said no bones were broken, but he thought she must have torn something inside. Her hip doesn't seem to want to get better."

She shrugged, her fingers trembling as she remembered the first days after the accident when her mother was black and blue and in so much pain.

"I'm sorry," Adam murmured. "I'm sure it's been difficult for you."

Chas stared at the pies for a moment, breathing slowly, letting peace fill her before she lifted her face and smiled at Adam. "The worst part has been seeing her pain. As for the rest of it—all my life I've been taught God is as close as a prayer and His angels ready to minister to us. It was a thought that carried me through my childhood."

At this Adam nodded.

"But this situation made it more than a teaching. I wouldn't have traded it for anything," she added.

Caught in his blue-eyed gaze, something inside her responded to his unblinking intensity. Not a word was spoken, yet she felt a volume had been said.

"It's as if living makes life real," he said, nodding slowly.

It was exactly how she felt. Life was not chasing adventure or seeing new and exciting things. It was experienced in the living of every day to the full. She tried to make it the motto of her life.

"But—"

He smiled. "I know. You thought I had to roam the edges of the world to find meaning for my life. But that's not how it is. Sure, I want to see and touch those far places. I want to witness the making of history." He shook his head. "But I know that is not where or how life gets meaning."

"So what have you discovered gives life meaning?" Chas realized she'd been holding her breath so that her words sounded airy.

Emma sat with knife poised motionless over the basin, her eyes wide and fixed on Adam's back. Her surprise was natural. Chas herself wondered how the conversation had taken such a serious turn.

"That's easy," Adam answered, his expression warming. "Meaning and satisfaction come from inside oneself." He tilted his head to one side. "It's in knowing that all is right with the world because God is in control, and all is right with me because I am one of His children."

Her jaw slackened. Chas couldn't tear her gaze from the look of peace and assurance in his face. Deep inside, something unfolded as she recognized a faith matching her own.

"That's it exactly," she murmured.

Emma's knife clanged against the basin. "My! To listen to you two, one would think life should be a safe, narrow existence." She grunted. "Adam, I thought you of all people would understand the need for something more."

His eyes lingered on Chas a moment longer before he turned toward the younger girl. "I guess there's no point in my saying there's no place in life for adventure." He grinned at her. "Life would certainly be dull without it. But that's not what I'm talking about." He faced Chas again. "With or without that sort of thing, peace is found inside."

"Hmph! Sometimes I think there's a tad too much peace around here," Emma retorted.

Chas had been working as they talked, and now she fluted the edges of the crusts and slashed the tops. She grabbed a pie in each hand and eased around Adam to slip them in the oven. Turning to get the other two pies, she almost collided with him where he stood at her elbow with a pie in each hand.

"Thank you," she half-whispered, glad of the excuse to lower her head and hide her confusion as she slid them into the oven. She closed the oven door, wiping her hands on her apron and straightening a towel on the handle. She had no choice then but to face him.

His expression sober, he studied her face. "You've grown from a girl into a woman." His gaze lingered on her nose, then dropped to her chin before circling back to her eyes. "A fine woman. But in many ways I think you're still the same— serene and inscrutable."

His assessment both surprised and dismayed her. It made her sound like one of Mother's lifeless statues—like the one by the window of the dining room—smooth, cool porcelain.

Adam sighed. "I better get back to the store before Father thinks I've gotten lost." He dusted a speck of flour from his pants. "Thanks again. I'll be seeing you."

He turned and strode out the door before Chas could pull her thoughts together.

Emma watched her curiously. "Exactly how well did you know Adam?"

Chas shrugged, busying herself with cleaning up the table. "I barely remember him. He was"—she paused—"oh, probably three or four years older. Of course I knew who he was. After all, it's a small town."

Emma set the pot of potatoes aside ready to put on the stove when the time came. "He sure seemed to know a lot about you."

"I'm surprised he even remembers me."

"You must have done something for him to have such a definite opinion of what you were like."

Chas scowled as she tried to think of all she knew of Adam.

"He liked to draw," she mused out loud. "I remember him getting into trouble at school because he would waste his time drawing instead of listening." She chuckled. "I do recall he liked to see things real close so he could draw them better. One time he tried to see a beehive closer and got stung rather badly for his efforts."

Emma's eyes grew round. "Ouch."

"He swelled up all bumpy." She stared out the window at the memories from long ago. "Another time he climbed up a tree to look into a bird's nest." She gasped. "I remember now. He fell out of the tree and landed on top of Esther James and me." She giggled. "Esther was so mad I thought she would hurt him. She might have if he hadn't hidden."

Chas remembered the rest of the incident to herself. Esther had thought Adam ran toward the store, but he had ducked behind the fence. Chas had seen, but she hadn't told. Later that day, or perhaps it was the next day, he had come and thanked her for letting him escape and handed her a sheet of paper. He was gone before she could look at it. It was a drawing of her—one that made her look grown up and beautiful with her fair hair circling her face and a bouquet of wild flowers lifted to her chin. She had treasured the drawing for years, hoping she would someday be as beautiful as he had made her look. She thought for a moment. The drawing was probably still tucked away among her school items.

Chas turned away from the window. "I'll clean up the tea things and check on Mother."

Emma nodded. "I'll get this mess tidied up." Already she was heading for the door to throw the vegetable peelings on the garden.

Mrs. B had returned to her room, no doubt anxious to get back to her crocheting.

Mother sat in the chair, head tilted back, eyes closed. She heard her daughter approaching and opened her eyes.

Chas's heart tightened at the weary lines around her mother's eyes. "Come, Mama—I'll help you to your room. I think you should take a little rest before supper."

"*Merci*, my dear."

She let her daughter help her to her feet, and together they headed down the hall toward the bedroom. She stifled a groan as Chas helped her lie down.

"I don't know what I would do without you, Chastity," she murmured.

Chas pulled a quilt over her shoulders and brushed her hair back from her forehead. Here and there a few silver strands showed up in her mother's black hair, still thick and luxuriant. Again Chas wondered how her mother could be so dark-haired while she had hair as blond as bottled sunshine. The father she never knew must have been fair-haired.

At one time she had resented her hair coloring. People would touch her head and make comments about it—"angel wings," "goose down." But as she had grown older, people had stopped touching, and her hair had become thick and heavy, no longer flying about her face like thistledown. Chas had learned to accept her fairness, tying her hair at the back of her neck and, for the most part, paying little attention to it.

She kissed her mother's brow, her hands lingering. Her insides tightened until she could barely breathe. Her mother had already suffered so much pain with her hip.

Please, God, don't let her suffer anymore.

Mother sighed and closed her eyes. Chas slipped away to the kitchen.

"I'm going to Doc Johnson's and ask him to drop by to see Mother this evening," she told Emma. "Keep an eye on the pies, will you?"

"Of course. Is she in a great deal of pain?"

"She's trying to hide it, but she can scarcely move." Chas took a trembling breath. "I'm guessing she's undone everything."

"Just when she was getting better." Emma shook her head. "It's too bad. But you run along. Take your time." She smiled. "Take the 'long' way home. I can manage here."

Chas laughed. "I know you can." Emma had proven herself capable since the day she walked into the kitchen shortly after her mother's accident.

Chas stepped into the sunshine, lifting her face to the warmth. She would never have managed running the boardinghouse without Emma's help, not after Stella, the woman who had worked for her mother for years, had walked out in a huff declaring she would not work for a young girl. Although dismayed by Stella's leaving, Chas had smiled at being described as a young girl, for she felt she was well on her way to being an old maid. She reached the sidewalk, squinting against the brightness of the sky. It was beginning to look as if she would spend her life running the boardinghouse for her mother—doomed to be a spinster for life.

For about the space of a heartbeat, disappointment swelled in her chest. Then she smiled, comforting herself with the assurance that God would work things out for her good.

In Your time, Lord—in Your time.

The streets of Willow Creek rang with summer. Chastity's steps held a little spring as she made her way to the doctor's office. A few minutes later, after leaving a message with Doc Johnson's nurse, she stood on the steps outside his office.

Across the street and up a few buildings was Silverhorn's Mercantile. At that moment Chas saw Adam walk out of the store, with Jack following him. She couldn't make out what they were saying, but Jack was waving his arms and talking rapidly. Adam ruffled his younger brother's hair and nodded. Together they stepped into the shadowed doorway of the storeroom. Chas waited a moment longer, but they didn't reappear. Soon she could hear the sound of hammering. Adam must not be wasting any time getting to work on his shop.

Rather than turn her steps toward home, she decided to do as Emma had suggested and take the long way down the side streets past the elegant homes of Willow Creek's prosperous businessmen. She thought the three-story, turreted house and the two replicas further down the street were beautiful. The yards were finely manicured. But in her mind they were not places to spend time dreaming about, and she hummed under her breath as she strolled along the pleasant streets.

She glanced about her, noting how the flowers were thriving in one yard and admiring the new green trim on a house across the street. She breathed deeply of the familiar scents of lilacs, a freshly mowed lawn and the distant underlying odor of a nearby farm. She had never been more than a few miles from this town in her whole life, and somehow she couldn't imagine why anyone would want to wander very far away.

She turned a corner. Her steps quickened until she neared the end of the block and slowed down. She took two more steps, then stopped, touching the white picket fence and staring at the low white house, surrounded by perennials and low bushes. Tall poplars lined one side of the yard, with a stately spruce forming the backdrop. A narrow veranda ran the length of the house.

After a moment she made her way past the gate to the corner of the fence and turned down the sidewalk. She peered into the backyard, where a stone pathway led to a tiny lattice arbor under which stood a white wrought iron table and two matching chairs. A book lay turned over on the table, a cup beside it.

Her heart beat calmly when she finally turned away, a smile tugging at her lips as she made her way toward the boardinghouse.

two

Emma carried in the gravy while Chas came behind with the potatoes. She checked to see if everything was in place, then pulled out the chair at her mother's right.

As soon as she was seated, Mother took her hand. "Let's pray."

They all bowed their heads, and there was a moment of silence.

They had offered a blessing that way since Chas was nine years old—when Mr. Brownlee died and her mother inherited the boardinghouse.

At the time, curious about the change from her mother's asking the blessing, Chas had waited until they were in their own rooms, the rooms where Mr. and Mrs. Brownlee had previously slept, before she asked, "Mama, why did we have to pray like that?"

Her mother sat down beside her on the edge of the bed that had been moved from the upstairs bedroom. "Some of those men at our table would feel belittled to have a woman ask the blessing. This way nobody needs to be offended."

"Amen." Mother's word was the signal to begin, as hands reached for the dishes and spooned the food onto their plates.

Chas looked around the table.

Mrs. B sat across from her, where her mother could unobtrusively give whatever help she needed.

Next to Mrs. B was Beryl Hanes, her fan of dark curls emphasizing her plumpness. Beryl had been with them almost a year and worked at the bank. Catching Chas watching her, Beryl smiled.

Chas smiled back before continuing her quick assessment

24

of the others at the table.

Carl and Orsby Knutsen were newcomers. They had come from the farm a month ago and managed to find jobs on the section crew of the Canadian Pacific Railway. Still too shy to say anything in front of the others, they kept their heads down, focusing on their food.

Louise, secretary to a lawyer, was the last one on that side. She had been at the boardinghouse a little longer than Beryl. Louise was tall, blond, and willowy. Chas admired her bearing. Even her name was elegant—Louise Leishman.

Mr. Elias maintained his post at the end of the table with quiet dignity.

Emma sat next to him so she could watch to see if anything was needed at that end of the table.

Between Chas and Emma were Roy Vandenberg, who worked in the drugstore, and John Nelson, who worked in the land titles office. They had been living in the boardinghouse since last fall.

Michael sat beside Chas. Besides Emma, who lived with her folks at the far edge of town, Michael, a teacher, was the only one who didn't live in the house. But he was regular enough not to be thought of as a guest.

"I stopped in at Silverhorn's on my way home from work," Louise said in her cool, controlled tones. "The place was in quite a state of confusion. I believe the older son, Adam, has returned. Seems he's going to set up a photography shop in conjunction with the store."

Beryl leaned forward. "I was there too. And I saw the most amazing painting. You should have seen it." Her look included everyone. "It was huge. Even bigger than the one over the fireplace in the other room."

Chas knew she meant the guardian angel picture.

"What was it of?" Roy asked.

Roy had a need to know the particulars of everything. One time the discussion had been about a trip to Banff, and someone said it looked like Main Street sprung from the roots of

Cascade Mountain. Roy kept asking how high the mountain was and how far it was from the administrative building to the Banff Springs Hotel until everyone became quite annoyed.

But this time Beryl showed no annoyance. "It was of a mountain but nothing like the mountains we have here. It was all ice with light glistening off it and the sun setting—or maybe it was rising, for all I know. Anyway, it tinted parts of the snow with pink." She waved a hand. "But pink isn't the right name for the way the color shone."

Louise broke in. "Goodness, Beryl. You make it sound mystical."

"It was. You'll have to see for yourself."

"Where was this mountain?" Roy demanded.

"I asked. Mr. Silverhorn said it was in the Yukon. Then his son—"

"Adam," Louise supplied.

"Yes, Adam. He came in and said it was Muir Glacier." She sighed. Her hands lay still, and she got a dreamy look on her face. "He said to think of Niagara Falls frozen stiff, add about thirty feet to its height, and you begin to imagine what it's really like." For a moment she stared across the table at nothing in particular, then laughed a little. "It was very romantic."

Wondering if she meant the painting or Adam, Chas saw that everyone was caught up in Beryl's description. Even the Knutsen brothers lifted their heads and listened as if it was as important as food.

"Muir Glacier then. Not really a mountain—is that what you're saying?" Roy had to know.

Beryl shrugged. "Looked like a mountain to me. A mountain covered with ice."

"Remember she said the Yukon? Isn't it always frozen?" Even John, who usually avoided taking part in discussions unless they had to do with crops or farm prices, was drawn into the conversation.

Michael spoke up. "They have summer too. The sun shines twenty-four hours a day."

"Adam was here today," Emma said. "He told us about his travels."

Emma made it sound as if they had been visited by royalty.

"Here?"

"Did he say where he'd been?"

"Who is this Adam?"

They were asking so many questions that Emma waved her hands in the air. "I wasn't the only one who saw him. Chas, Mr. Elias, Mrs. B, Miz LaBlanc—they all saw him. In fact, he picked Miz LaBlanc off the floor."

The young people turned to Chas's mother.

"Why were you on the floor?" Roy demanded.

"I fell."

Beryl reached for her hand. "Are you all right?"

Before her mother could answer, Chas said, "She's hurt her hip again."

Everyone but Mrs. B, muddling over her meat, looked at Mother.

"I'm so sorry," Louise said gently.

"I suppose this means you won't be wanting your job back anytime soon?" Michael murmured close to Chas's ear.

"Shh." She shook her head, not wanting her mother to hear.

He leaned closer and whispered, "We'll talk later."

She nodded and turned back to the conversation.

Emma told about Adam's visit. "He said he would give Miz LaBlanc a private showing of his pictures."

"I'm sure he didn't mean anything as formal as that," Mother said. "And he didn't mean only me."

Roy reached for the potatoes before he asked, "So he's planning to stay?"

Emma shrugged. "I guess. Sort of."

"Until something more exciting comes up." Chas smiled in an attempt to take any sting from her words.

Roy demanded to know how long Adam had been gone and where.

Emma did her best to supply the answers.

Beryl fairly bounced on her chair. "I heard him tell his father he was going to display some pictures from the Klondike. Doesn't it sound exciting?"

"I wonder if he would let the children see them." Michael strained forward. "Think of how educational it would be." He turned to Chas. "What do you think, Chas? Do you think he would give a talk at the school?"

"That's a good idea. Why not ask him?" She pushed back from the table. "I'll get the pie."

Emma gathered up the plates and serving dishes as Chas sliced pie and spooned on whipped cream.

When she returned, the conversation still centered on Adam Silverhorn and his adventures. Chas held her tongue as she passed the dessert. She longed to bring everyone back to reality, but everything she thought of sounded like the words of a bitter old maid. She certainly didn't want people to have that impression, but all this excitement about a man who had left his home and family without a backward look seemed uncomfortably out of proportion. It made normal life appear narrow and dull, which it wasn't. Life was full and satisfying.

Like now, for instance.

Chas slid Mrs. B's plate under her arm and set the fork where she would find it without searching. She felt pleasure in seeing Mrs. B happy; in the grateful comments of the boarders as they sampled the pie; in the closeness of her "family." She met Michael's dark brown gaze and smiled. No, she couldn't imagine why anyone would feel the need to seek adventure elsewhere.

⁊ə

Chas and Emma carried the dishes back to the kitchen and cleaned off the dining room table. Chas wanted to do the dishes right away, but Michael pulled out a handful of papers. "I thought you might like to read some of the essays the class wrote."

"Emma, I'll be a minute." She dried her hands and sat down again, taking the papers Michael offered. He often brought assignments and tests for her to help check, along with regular news of the class she had taught until two years ago—the class that was now his responsibility. "What was the topic?"

" 'The Importance of Being Trustworthy.' "

"Good topic." She read the first one. "Annie's developing her expression."

Michael leaned back. "She's improving, but I'm having a hard time deciding how to grade the essay."

Chas straightened. "But why?"

He pulled his tie to the center of his shirt and folded his long arms across his chest before he answered. "It's written well enough, but I don't think she's properly addressed the topic."

With a puzzled look, Chas read the essay through again. "She talks about truth a lot. Isn't that being trustworthy?"

"True. But she's missed the biggest part—doing what you say you will and what others are counting on from you. We talked about this a long time before I gave them this assignment."

Still feeling as if they were talking about different things, Chas asked, "So how did you explain trustworthiness to a group of ten and eleven year olds?"

"I told them about my brother, Timothy, and me. When we were growing up, I tried to be honest about some of the things I felt, and it was perceived as a failure to do what I should. On the other hand, Timothy did what he was told while never agreeing with anything my parents believed. They felt they could count on him. And I learned my lesson: Sometimes it doesn't matter how we feel inside. We should simply do what's expected."

His reasoning troubled Chas. "You make it sound like believing and doing are different things. Isn't that hypocrisy of the worst sort?"

He shook his head. "Not exactly. Sometimes you have to do things even when you don't like or agree with them. Take yourself as an example."

She drew back. "Me?" When had she acted out of insincerity?

"Certainly. You were happy as a teacher. You had plans."

He read the denial in her expression and added, "You know you did. You told me how you hoped to get yourself a little house someday."

She wanted to explain, but he continued before she had a chance.

"Then you had to quit teaching to look after this place." His gaze swept the room, then touched on the ceiling including the rooms upstairs. "So what do you do? You smile and do your work as if it's all that matters."

"You make it sound as if inside I'm a quivering mass of resentment and unfulfilled dreams."

He didn't answer, only held her gaze.

"But I'm not. I was disappointed at first, but I wasn't unhappy about it. I'm not unhappy now."

"You certainly have maintained a good face, and that's truly admirable. Even today, after your mother fell again, you smiled and acted as if it didn't matter that you're stuck here even longer."

"Michael." She couldn't believe he had misjudged her so. Michael of all people. She began again on a quieter note. "I'm not pretending—putting on a good face, as you say. I'm content. And, yes, happy. Happy to be helping my mother and doing a good job running the house. But more than that, I'm convinced God is in control. He will work out what is best for me. He is totally trustworthy."

"You're right, of course. But I wanted the children to express something more than simply being honest. There's more to it."

She nodded. "I realize that. But shouldn't what we believe reveal itself in how we act?" Not waiting for him to answer, she bent her head and focused on the next essay.

It was true she had thought her life would be different. Before her mother's accident, Chas took it for granted the older woman would manage the boardinghouse until she was too old to do so and then sell it. And Chas would teach until—she closed her eyes and breathed deeply. Her dreams had included love and marriage and a quiet little home that sheltered only her, her husband, and their children.

But she had fought her disappointment and won. She would leave her future in God's hands. And above all, she would not allow herself to become a bitter old maid with a razor-sharp tongue. She pictured Pastor Simpson's sister, Martha, with her puckered mouth and sour-apple comments and shuddered. Even if she never married, she vowed she would not let bitterness turn her into another Martha Simpson.

Forcing her mind back to the papers in her hands, she read young Joel's comments about the dire results of being untrustworthy and chuckled.

The next piece belonged to Jack Silverhorn, and she read it with sharpened interest.

"Being trustworthy," she read, "means being honest all the time even when it's hard. It means being honest in what you say and do. It means doing what you said you will even when you change your mind and don't want to do it. It means always coming back. It's important to be trustworthy so people know what to expect from you."

She put her finger on her chin. *Always coming back.* Did Jack mean Adam, the brother he had met for the first time a few days ago? She hated to think of Jack's being hurt when Adam decided to leave again.

Michael pulled out another sheaf of papers, and Chas knew he was settling in for a night of correcting papers and working on lesson plans. But beyond the door, Emma rattled the dishes.

"Michael, I have to help Emma."

He barely glanced up. "Let her do it. It's her job."

"Not really," Chas said, sighing.

Emma had volunteered to extend her day until the supper dishes were done, but Chas knew Emma had a life apart from her job and would be anxious to go home or out with friends.

"But I thought we would work on the lesson plan for next week."

He looked up with a pleading, wide-eyed look she found hard to resist, and she wondered, not for the first time, if he did it on purpose.

"If you want to wait until I'm finished—"

He grinned. "I have nothing else to do."

Chas hurried to the kitchen. "I'm sorry," she told Emma. "You go on home. I'll finish up."

Emma shook her head. "I'll stay, or you won't finish until time for bed." She plunged her hands into the hot dishwater. "Doesn't Michael realize you're busy?"

Chas shrugged. "I enjoy hearing about the children."

"I know you do, but he should have seen you had extra to do today."

Her mother had needed help back to her room. Mrs. B was fretful and wanting to talk. And there was still the dough to set to rise for tomorrow's bread. "It's just one of those days." She dried the dishes as fast as Emma washed them. "But then I guess every day has its share of good and bad."

"I guess overall it was a good day."

"I take it you mean Adam Silverhorn?" The younger girl was blinded by the man.

Emma sniffed. "You know I do. Stop pretending you weren't impressed."

"But I wasn't."

"You need your eyes checked."

Chas smiled. "Maybe I saw more than you think."

"So you're admitting he's handsome as a king?"

Chas's smile widened. "I didn't mean his looks."

Emma straightened to look at her. "What do you mean?"

"I saw a man who lives for adventure. How long do you think he'll be happy to hang around Willow Creek?"

Emma shrugged. "What difference does it make? I intend to enjoy his company as long as he's here—and see his pictures and ask him about his travels. If he goes again, at least I won't have wasted the opportunity. If he stays, so much the better."

Chas didn't answer. Emma's words held an element of

truth, yet it wasn't enough for her.

Emma grabbed Chas by the shoulders, her wet hands making two damp spots, and pushed her toward the window. "What do you see out there?" she demanded.

Dusk had fallen, and the yard lay in gray shadows. "I can't see much. It's dark."

"You know what's out there. Tell me."

Chas shrugged. "Trees and grass and lilac bushes."

"Exactly. And how long do lilacs last?"

"Not nearly long enough."

"That's not the point. The point is, you enjoy them the little while they're in bloom." Emma returned to scrubbing the roaster.

"It's not the same."

Chas looked out for a minute longer. Trees and flowers were supposed to change with the seasons. She sighed and turned back to the chores. Michael was right. She longed for other things in life.

"Of course there's a very big difference between a bunch of lilacs and Adam." Emma sighed loudly to indicate her opinion in Adam's favor. "But you can enjoy it just the same and let it go when you have to." She paused. "As long as you don't fall in love."

Chas couldn't help the way she pulled back. "That would be begging for trouble."

Emma shrugged. "A person could always go with him on his adventures. Think of all the things you'd get to see."

It was so far removed from what she wanted that Chas's mouth went dry at the very thought. "I don't understand why anyone would want to go to those places."

Emma studied her. "Don't you find them interesting?"

"Oh, yes, I find them immensely interesting. They're like the different flowers of the seasons. Each season to be enjoyed and admired. It's just—" She didn't know how to explain that the mere thought of wandering from place to place, living from day to day, left her with an empty echo inside.

"Then I suggest you don't fall in love with Adam Silverhorn."

"You can count on that."

"Chas, are you finished yet?" Michael called from the other room.

"In a minute." She pushed back a strand of hair clinging to her cheek. She still had the dough to mix and a list of small things—like watering the African violets on the window ledge, putting away the clutter on the cupboard, wiping the table, checking to see if everything was handy for the morning. But those things could wait. It wasn't every night Michael called. Not quite.

She flipped off her apron. "You go on home now," she said to Emma. "I'll see you in the morning."

Emma shook her head. "Everything doesn't have to be done tonight."

"I know." Chas waited until Emma closed the door before she hurried to the dining room. "I'm sorry, Michael, but I'm finished now."

"Don't worry about it." He sat at the table, a fan of papers before him. "I understand." He grinned up at her. "It takes a lot of work to look after this place, and you do it very well. You should be proud of the job you do."

Tension slid from her shoulders. "Thank you. I like making sure things are well taken care of and doing little extras that make a difference."

"Just don't overdo it. You're only one person."

"I know."

He pulled out the chair next to him. They'd had this discussion before. She had explained how important it was to keep up the tradition her mother had started of running a boarding-house that provided more than a room and meals. Her mother had drummed into her head from her earliest memories that they could never be certain of the identity of the people who lived in their rooms.

"Remember—some could even be angels we're entertaining unaware," she had said.

Chas lowered her head to hide a smile. She had to admit that to the best of her knowledge she had never fed an angel, but the idea did make the work more satisfying.

As if reading her mind, Michael said, "Your mother places far too much emphasis on this angel business. A person can't turn around without running into a statue or a painting of one."

Chas laughed. "It's pretty hard to ignore, isn't it?"

"Downright impossible. It doesn't take all these paintings and things to be reminded of the angel's gift." He grabbed her hand, sending warm waves through her body. "One only has to look at you."

Chas knew her cheeks had blushed pink, and she shifted on her chair. With her free hand, she plucked at the papers on the table. "Michael, you're making me blush."

He squeezed her hand. "It's very becoming."

She returned his squeeze, relaxing under his gentle teasing. "You always make me feel better, you know."

He nodded. "Part of my job."

"I suppose the ad said, 'Besides taking over a classroom of nine to twelve year olds, the applicant must be willing to keep former teacher informed of her students' progress and provide cheer and encouragement to said teacher.' "

He shrugged. "You have your standards for your job; I have mine."

She looked deep into his eyes, liking the steady warmth she saw, finding calmness settling into her bones. Michael was good for her. Steady as a rock. He would never pull up stakes and head for some far port in search of adventure. Not like Adam.

She blinked. *Where had that come from?*

"I thought of introducing some new arithmetic concepts next week. The grade-six class is ready to go on to. . ."

They spent a pleasant half hour discussing different exercises for the class before the bell sounded at the front door.

Chas hurried to answer it.

Doc Johnson, round as a toad, stood on the porch. He carried with him the slight odor of formaldehyde and disinfectant. "How's your mother? I understand she took another fall." His jowls shook as he talked. With a heavy tread, he stepped inside and hung his hat and jacket on a hook. "I warned her to take it easy."

"She isn't good at taking orders."

Doc chuckled, making his whole body jiggle. "She's always had a mind of her own." He rubbed his hands together a moment before picking up his worn black bag. "Though in all truth, it's what's made her such a strong woman. Now where is she?"

Chas waved down the hall. "In her room. I'll take you."

She led the way, pausing at the door. "Mother, Doc Johnson is here. I asked him to have a look at you."

Mother lay on her bed reading her Bible. She glanced over her glasses at the doctor. "Samuel, you needn't have bothered."

Doc stepped into the room. "Well, I'm already here, so let's have a look at what you've done to yourself."

"I'll be back in a few minutes." Chas pulled the door closed and hurried back to the dining room. "It's Doc. He's with Mother right now."

Michael shuffled the papers into a neat pile. "I'll be on my way."

She nodded. She really did need to look after things. She followed him to the door. "Thank you, Michael. It was nice to have your company."

"Saturday then?"

"Of course." It was a long-standing arrangement—every Wednesday and Saturday for supper, and church on Sunday with dinner afterward.

"I hope it's nothing serious with your mother."

"Me too."

They stood at the door, the silence between them as comfortable as a pair of worn slippers. He smiled at her, said, "See you then," and left.

" 'Bye." Chas pulled the door closed, her gaze resting on her hand curled around the knob, unable to identify the unsettled feeling in her stomach. She wished Michael had kissed her, but then he never had.

Pushing back her thoughts, she straightened her shoulders and hurried down the hall to knock on her mother's door.

"Come in," Mother called.

Doc sat on the edge of the bed, folding his stethoscope into his bag. He waited for Chas to close the door before he spoke. "Marie, I'd have to say you've probably undone all the good you accomplished over the last two years." He shook his head, his jowls swaying. "As I said before, you've torn a muscle or ligament or something. It's reluctant to get better."

Chas listened.

"I could suggest a trip to the city, where you could have surgery, but—"

Mother pushed herself up on her pillows. "It will get better, though, won't it, Samuel?"

Doc Johnson cleared his throat with the sound of a bull frog in a muddy swamp. "Given time. Lots of time. I'm not one to say—sometimes things seem to improve when we least expect them to."

"How long?" Mother demanded. "How long will it take?"

The doctor shrugged. "There's always hope. You should never lose hope. I've seen my share of miracles."

"Samuel, you're waffling."

He heaved his bulk to his feet. "No doubt you'll have to put in another two years at the very least. Then there's your age."

She drew back. "What about my age?"

"All I'm saying is, you aren't as young as you used to be." He handed Chas a slip of paper. "Take this to the drugstore tomorrow and get some more tablets for the pain."

Chas walked him to the door. "Doc, how much chance do you give her of getting back on her feet?"

He shifted into his jacket and parked his hat on his round

head. "My guess, and it's only a guess, is she'll gradually improve—if she takes it easy. But she'll never be strong again. As to running this house—" He shook his head. "I'll stop in again in a day or two. Call me if her pain gets severe."

After he left, Chas leaned on the door. Even though Doc Johnson had hedged his predictions, Chas understood what he refused to say: Mother would never be able to manage the boardinghouse again.

For two years she had willingly, happily done her job, always clinging to the knowledge, the hope, that at some point her mother would take over the task again.

Now she was faced with a harsher reality.

And she knew she must talk to her mother about it.

She silently prayed for wisdom as she returned to her mother's bedside.

"It doesn't sound too hopeful, does it, Mama?"

Her mother held a tiny angel carved from ivory. "I haven't given up yet."

"I would be disappointed if you did."

Squaring her shoulders, she faced the older woman. "Doc doesn't seem to think you'll ever be strong enough to run the boardinghouse again."

Mother's gaze veered to Chas's face. "Is that a fact?"

Chas refused to blink. "That's what he says."

"What if I prove him wrong?" Her voice was soft, but Chas recognized the stubborn lines on her face.

"I hope you do." She paused. "But it might take a very long time."

"Ah. But what seems long to you might seem but a passing thing to me." Her gaze had dropped back to the small ivory angel. "Who knows? Perhaps I'll get a miracle." Suddenly her dark eyes flashed at Chas. "I've had my share of them, you know."

"I know." Chas pulled a chair close and perched on the edge, leaning close to her mother. She waited for her hands to grow still, until she was sure she had her complete attention. "Mother, have you given any thought to selling the boardinghouse?"

The older woman pulled back and gave a little scream.

Chas half rose, not knowing if it was the question that had given her mother pain or if the sudden movement had sent a spasm through her hip.

Mother shook her head, and Chas sank back.

"Chastity LaBlanc. How could you even ask such a thing?" Her mother clutched the angel. "This has been my home for twenty-five years. It's the only home you've ever known. Why, this is where a miracle led me." She tilted her chin. "No. I will not sell the boardinghouse. I'm not prepared to roll over and play dead. Not yet. Not by a long way."

"I don't mean for you to give up. I thought we could get a little house together, just the two of us. We'd have time to enjoy the things we've never had time for."

"And how would we live?" her mother asked abruptly. "Have you thought of that?"

Chas lifted her shoulders and let them drop again. "I could go back to teaching. And you'd have the money from the sale of this place. We would do all right."

Mother turned to her, studying her long and hard before speaking. "Have you been so unhappy here?" she whispered. "Have I done the wrong thing in raising you this way?"

"Oh, no, Mother." She grasped her mother's small, cool hand. "I've been happy. I still am. My life has been enriched by living here—seeing so many people and learning what pleases them. It's just—" She stood to her feet and paced to the end of the bed, then faced her mother. "I'm not unhappy. I'm not. I know God will take care of me and my future. But"—she sighed—"I don't want to live here the rest of my life. I don't want to run this house until the day I die."

"Now you're being melodramatic. No one expects you to stay here until you die. I just need you to keep things going until I'm back on my feet. Can you do that for me?"

Chas's shoulders sagged. "Of course I will. You know you can count on me."

"I know I can, *ma cherie.*" She held out a hand. "Come here."

Chas went to her side and allowed her mother to pull her down on the edge of the bed. "I know a couple of years seem a long time when you're young, but it isn't very long in view of a lifetime."

"I suppose not."

"I'll be better much faster than you think."

"I hope you are—for your sake, not mine."

Mother wrapped her arms around Chas. "I believe I'm doing the right thing. You know I wouldn't do anything I thought would hurt you."

"I know."

"You're the best thing that ever happened to me in my whole life, Child. I love you."

Chas grinned. "Am I better than an angel?"

Mother chuckled. "Better by far. You're the gift of an angel." She paused. *"Ma cherie,* that is not quite correct. I know children are a gift of God, but in your case—"

Knowing how it upset her mother to talk about the past, Chas hugged her. "You're the best mother a girl could ever want. I love you lots."

Her mother gave her a little push. "Now away with you. Let your old mother rest."

Chas sighed. "I've still got bread dough to mix up. Then I'll be back, and we can read together." They always read the Bible together at bedtime.

Her mother smiled. "I'll be here."

Chas hurried from the room. She sang as she worked, but as she pounded and turned the dough, working it from a sticky mass to a smooth, elastic ball, a tear surprised her, trickling down her cheek and dripping off her chin. She dashed it away with the back of her wrist.

three

Mr. Elias came through the door as Chas handed Mrs. B the cream and sugar. Mother was already sitting in her chair, sipping from her cup.

Chas had been up once in the night to give her mother a tablet for pain. She had managed to persuade her to take breakfast in bed, but she had refused to stay there for lunch. Seeing her face smooth, her eyes clear, the tightness across Chas's temples relaxed.

Her mother was strong and stubborn, traits that had stood her in good stead throughout her life. Perhaps she would, as she predicted, prove Doc Johnson wrong.

The bell at the back door clanged.

"I'll get it," Emma called from the kitchen, where she was getting scones.

Chas wasn't expecting any deliveries and wondered who could be calling. She didn't have to wonder long for Emma hurried into the room with the plate of scones in her hands and Adam at her heels.

"I've come for tea, if I may," he said.

"Why, how nice. Sit here beside me." Mother indicated the chair at her side. "Chastity, Dear, get Adam some tea." She beamed as Adam pulled the chair closer.

"Of course," Chas murmured.

Mrs. B leaned forward for a better look.

Emma sprang to Adam's side, offering a scone.

Even Mr. Elias edged forward a couple of inches in his chair, his gaze lingering on the stack of papers in Adam's hand.

Chas grinned. Adam certainly had a way of making his presence felt.

He looked up as she handed him his tea and caught the amusement in her expression. For a moment they regarded each other openly. Then he shrugged and smiled.

"I thought they might enjoy seeing some pictures."

"Adam, how lovely of you to remember." Mother refused the scone Emma offered.

"We'll enjoy tea first," Adam said. "Then I'll show you what I've brought."

Mother made a wry face. "You're much too astute for a boy." She turned to Emma. "I've changed my mind. I'll have a scone after all."

Emma chuckled. "Miz LaBlanc, don't you go letting him turn your head."

Mother waved her away. "It's too late for me, but if I were your age"—she paused—"or Chastity's—"

"Mother!" Chas knew her cheeks were flaming pink. She turned a desperate look at Adam. "She thinks she's being funny."

Adam laughed—a low, pleasant sound—and met her gaze, his sparkling blue eyes never blinking. Then he turned away, allowing Chas to draw a deep breath.

"How are you today, Mrs. Banner?" he asked, raising his voice and leaning close.

"You're that nice young boy from the store, aren't you?" She squinted to get a better look. "You're very much like your mother, aren't you?"

"Yes, I am. Are you well today?"

"I remember when she first came here with her new husband and a little boy with a thatch of blond hair and eyes so blue—" She leaned closer, peering into Adam's right eye and then his left. "They're still as blue as God's great sky." She leaned back, satisfied.

Adam grinned. "Thank you, Mrs. B." He turned to Mr. Elias. "Good day, Sir."

Mr. Elias nodded. "It's a fine day."

"You'll be going out later to enjoy the sun?"

"I take my daily constitutional every afternoon, rain or shine."

"Ah. But how much more pleasant on a day like today."

Mr. Elias tucked his chin in. "I've learned to forge ahead whatever the weather."

Adam studied him. "I'm guessing you were a soldier."

Mr. Elias pulled himself taller in his chair. "I was indeed in Her Royal Majesty's service for twenty years."

Chas gaped at the pair. Adam had discovered in five minutes something she hadn't known in the five years Mr. Elias had been there.

"Where did you serve?"

"Mostly in the East Indies."

Adam nodded, his expression thoughtful. "Someday I'd like to talk to you about your experiences, if I may?"

"That would be fine." Mr. Elias settled back, looking pleased.

"Are we finished with tea?" Mother asked, and everyone murmured agreement.

Chas quickly gathered up the cups as Adam untied the strings around his sheaf of papers.

"I thought I'd give you an overview of what it was like to go to the Klondike." He pulled out a photo. "You could take several routes, depending on where you disembarked, but all were treacherous beyond imagination. This series of photos depicts what is probably the most famous route—the passage to Dyea and then over the Chilkoot Trail."

Adam handed Mother a photo, which she studied before passing it to Emma. He then handed another to Mother.

"Men faced the most incredible odds. The strong overcame them. The weak turned back—or, worse, simply sat down and quit. Then there were the weak of a different sort who took advantage of other men's desperation and profited from it."

Chas found herself drawn to the tale of men against the elements—weather, terrain that would stop a mountain goat—things at once beautiful and terrifying.

"This picture shows the city of tents on the shores of Lynn Canal. Thousands of people arrived there." He passed around more pictures. "This is a group of men, outfitted for the trail." He paused. "To reach the Klondike River, each man had to cross a formidable range of mountains."

Chas gasped as the enormity of the gold fever stared back at her in stark black and white. "It looks like half the population raced off in search of gold."

"The fervor these men displayed was incredible." Adam pointed to the picture in her hand. "These are the golden stairs."

She saw an unbroken line of men scaling a steep slope.

"The slope was thirty-five degrees, making it necessary for each man to walk so he bent over looking at his boots. It was a torturous climb."

Chas shook her head. "It's incredible."

Adam held up his hand. "That's only the beginning. At the top the Mounties had a border check. In order to be allowed any further, each man had to have two thousand pounds of supplies. You have to understand there were no supplies available until ships could navigate the frozen waterways. So each man had to carry in what he needed." He bent over the photo, his head close to Chas's. "A man could carry fifty pounds on his back. That meant he had to make the twenty-mile trip over this pass forty times."

"Forty times!" Chas stared into his blue eyes, dark and serious.

"Many men died trying to make it."

"But you made it." She couldn't take her eyes off him, thinking of the horrors he had faced as he forged his way to the Klondike. This was more than seeking adventure; it required the determination of a sort that awed her.

He shook his head. "I took the all-Canadian route. It had its own set of challenges." Finally he pulled his gaze away and straightened to address the whole room. "These photos I'm showing you now were not taken by me. They were taken by a man I met in the Klondike. I got them from him."

Curious about the tightness she heard in his voice, Chas asked, "Who was this man?"

"He was the man who taught me everything I know about photography. He was a very special person."

Suddenly Chas's desire to know more seemed insatiable. Who was this man? What had happened to him? What had he meant to Adam? And more. How had men survived such an ordeal? How many actually found gold? What about their families? But something in Adam's expression—a tightness around his eyes—made her wonder if he had painful memories he didn't wish to share, so she chose to keep her questions to herself.

The last of Adam's pictures had passed from hand to hand.

"Adam, those were truly wonderful," Mother said. "Thank you."

Emma sighed. "Now I'll know what people are talking about when they mention the Klondike gold rush and the Chilkoot Trail."

Mr. Elias nodded. "It's a wonderful documentary you have there, young fellow. I wish I had such a record of my own journeys."

"Yes, thank you, Adam," Chas said, her mind still transfixed by what she had seen and heard. It was a magical experience, like being transported to another time, another place.

"I can bring more pictures and maybe some sketches sometime, if you like. And maybe of other places." He gave a low chuckle. "I have ten years' worth of stories and pictures."

"We'd like that," Mother said for them all. "How wonderful to have such a collection."

Mr. Elias cleared his throat. "If you'll excuse me, I'll be on my way." He rose and marched to the door, his measured steps thudding up the stairs and then descending again as he headed outdoors.

Emma, clearing away the tea things, watched him through the window and then leaned over and spoke close to Chas's ear. "He's got a parcel with him again. What do you suppose he's up to?"

Chas frowned at Emma. If Mother overheard them discussing Mr. Elias's personal life, they would both be in for a scolding.

"Our boarders are entitled to their privacy," she had said over and over. "As long as they don't do anything illegal. We would then, of course, be obligated to report them to the authorities."

That was Emma's loophole. "How do we know what anybody's doing? For instance, maybe Mr. Elias is—I don't know—maybe he's making counterfeit bills."

Chas had laughed at her suggestion. "I suppose he sits up in his bedroom painstakingly drawing each bill."

"He could." Emma drew her brows together. "Or he could be making some other kind of forgery. He could be doing all sorts of things."

Chas had shaken her head. "Or he could be borrowing books from a friend."

At that Emma had pulled away. "That's real exciting."

Now Emma mumbled, "Makes you think, doesn't it?"

Ignoring her, Chas turned back to hear what her mother was saying to Adam. "You certainly have a fine collection of photos. I'm anxious to see more of them. And the sketches you keep mentioning."

Adam's gaze circled the room. "You have a fine collection yourself."

Mother followed the direction of his look as did Chas, her heart dropping like a stone as he studied the angel figurine in the window, then the painting over the fireplace, then the framed drawing next to the hall of an angel looking as if he were listening for a call. Penned underneath were words Chas knew by heart: "But if these beings guard you, they do so because they have been summoned by your prayers."

Mother nodded with a bright smile. "I've collected angels since before Chastity was born. They serve as a constant reminder to me that 'the angel of the LORD encampeth round about them that fear him, and delivereth them.' "

Adam looked at the older woman. "I sense a story."

"I'll say it again—you are much too discerning for a young man." She settled back.

Chas squeezed her hands together. She had heard the story many times throughout her life and was always uncomfortable when her mother told it. It made her feel like a spectacle. She edged forward in her chair, hoping she could slip out, but her mother lifted her hand.

"Stay, Chastity. You should hear this."

"I've heard it before, Mother," she said quietly.

"I know, but stay."

Her mother's gentle voice set Chas back in her chair more effectively than a brisk order. She clutched her hands together and refused to look up.

"I married young," Mother began, "and not wisely. I thought my husband was everything I'd dreamed of—a caring, principled man who would take gentle care of me." She took a deep breath. "Neither of us had much in the way of family, so it was easy for us to pull up stakes and move West."

Chas steeled herself for the next installment.

"I don't know if moving West changed him or if it revealed him for who he really was. He grew angry, demanding, and cruel. When I knew I was pregnant, I hid it, fearing what he would do." Her gaze rested on Chastity.

Her mother always found this part of her story painful, and Chas met her look, silently encouraging her and affirming her love.

"Your father's name was Simon LaBlanc."

Chas gripped her hands together so tightly her knuckles hurt. Never before had her mother given the name of her father or even said if LaBlanc was his name or her mother's maiden name.

"I promised to leave the past behind me when I came here," she had insisted when Chas questioned her.

"Simon LaBlanc," Chas repeated, her voice thin. "What was he like?"

"He was charming and handsome. His mother was Swedish, his father French. It's from his mother's side you get your coloring."

Her throat too tight to speak, Chas nodded.

"But he was a no-good scoundrel," her mother said with a sigh. "When he found out I was pregnant, he beat me." Her voice dropped to a whisper.

Adam cleared his throat. "You don't have to tell me. I didn't mean to pry into something personal."

Chas had forgotten he was there and blinked back the emotion rising in her eyes, striving to compose her face.

Mother waved aside his comment, addressing Chas directly. "I've wondered for a long time if I was right in keeping this from you. I decided a few days ago if someone were to ask me to tell them about the angels, I would take it as a sign to tell you." She turned to Adam. "It's a story most people around here have heard bits and pieces of. I'm not sure why, but having you here has given me the strength to tell Chastity about her father."

She continued. "He kicked me out and said he never wanted to see me again. He had hurt me so badly I was afraid I would lose my baby, who was, of course, Chastity." Her voice quivered. "I knew no one. I had no place to go. I had no money. All I wanted was to get away. Far, far away. So I started down the road. A couple picked me up and took me several miles. That night I slept by the edge of the road with nothing but my shawl to keep me warm. I headed out again as soon as it was light. I don't even know what direction I was going. I walked all day. Toward dark I was so weak I kept falling down." Never once did her gaze flicker from Chas's face. "I hadn't eaten in two days, and I was bleeding."

She took a deep breath. "Finally I just couldn't get up. I thought I was going to die. I no longer thought I believed in God, but I remember thinking, 'God, if You don't help me,

I'm finished.' " Her voice grew stronger. "That's when a buggy pulled up beside me. A young man came to me and lifted me into it. I seemed to float in his arms. He gave me some warm broth, washed my face and hands, and wrapped me in a warm quilt." She smiled. "I don't know if I slept or what, but we soon drove into town. The man stopped in front of a big house and took me to the door.

" 'You'll be safe here,' he said as he rang the bell. 'God wants you to know He sees your trouble and will surely rescue you. He wants you to understand how much He loves you.'

"And then the door opened. A sweet-faced older lady welcomed me as if she had sent me an invitation. When I turned around to thank the kind gentleman, he wasn't there, and there was no buggy in the street."

Mother smiled. "He had vanished into thin air.

"That's how I came to this house. Mr. and Mrs. Brownlee owned it. They took me in and cared for me until I regained my strength. I've lived here ever since."

The room was quiet.

"Mrs. Brownlee brought me my first angel," she added. "It's that little ivory one I keep by my bedside," she explained to Chas. "She said it was to remind me that when all hope is gone, we have endless hope in God's provision."

She sat back.

No one spoke.

Chas stole a look at Adam, wondering what he thought of the tale. Slowly he turned to face her, his eyes warm as a summer sky. "I always knew Chas had a special quality about her, and now I understand what it is: Her life has been touched in a special way."

"She's my gift."

Chas's cheeks grew warm, and she lowered her head to study her clenched hands. She knew the moment Adam shifted his gaze. She sucked in a deep breath to ease the tension crackling up her spine.

"That's a remarkable story, Miz LaBlanc. I don't know

when I've heard a more powerful one." He tidied his bundle of photos and stood. "It's been a lovely afternoon, and I thank you for your hospitality."

"Anytime, Adam. Consider it a standing invitation."

Chas stood as well. "Do you want help back to your bedroom?" she asked her mother.

"No, I'm quite comfortable here. If you'll bring me my Bible, I'll be fine."

"I'll do that. Then I think I'll go pick up some more of your pills." She turned to Adam. "Good-bye then. I enjoyed your stories of the Klondike."

"I'm glad."

Chas slipped from the room to get her mother's Bible. Adam was still there when she returned. Her eyebrows seemed to go up of their own accord.

He chuckled at her surprise. "Since we're headed in the same direction, I thought we might as well walk together."

She nodded, too confused to speak. Her emotions had been on a whirlwind ride from awe at the spectacular challenges the Klondikers faced, to reluctant admiration of Adam's experiences, to mouth-dropping surprise at her mother's revealing the name of Chas's father. She wasn't yet sure how she felt about it. She had never expected to be told and had long ago decided it didn't matter. Now that she had the information, she wasn't sure what she should do with it. She needed time to sort everything out.

Yet she wasn't reluctant for Adam's company. Something about him roused her curiosity. She had pegged him for an adventurer—bent on trying something new and exciting at every opportunity. But his stories of the Klondike had revealed something else—something she couldn't put her finger on.

"Are you ready?"

Chas smoothed a hand over her hair. She was acting as impressionable as Emma. "I'm ready."

They reached the drugstore first, and Adam accompanied

her inside and waited while Roy dispensed the pills Doc Johnson had ordered.

"Why don't you come and see what I'm doing at my shop?" Adam asked as they stepped back into the sunshine.

Curious, Chas agreed.

Inside the room Adam had claimed for his shop, Chas saw at once he had been hard at work. The mahogany wainscoting glistened with polish. The odor of calcimine stung her nostrils from the upper half of the walls with their soft green paint.

She stood in the middle of the floor and turned full circle. "I see you've been busy."

"I haven't done it alone. The whole family helped."

"I suppose they're hoping they can convince you to stay." She crossed her arms in front of her and squeezed tight.

His hands shoved into his pockets, Adam leaned against the door frame and gave a slow smile. "Chas, you talk as if I've only paused here to catch my breath. Do you think I would go to all this work if I was only visiting?"

Chas let her eyes circle the room. Stacks of framed pictures leaned against the wall. Crates waited to be unpacked or stored. "No, I suppose not." She brought her gaze back to Adam. "Do you mean to tell me you're planning to stay and put down roots, as they say?"

He smiled wider, light filling his eyes. "I have no immediate plans to go anywhere."

Chas wondered about the quickening of the pulse in her neck. She could barely breathe and glanced around the room again, wondering if someone had lit a fire in the stove. But there was no stove. No fire. "Are you saying you plan to stay here?"

He nodded. "I need a home base for my business."

"So you might take off again someday?"

He didn't answer. He simply stared at her until she looked down, mumbling, "I'm sorry. It's none of my business."

He sighed. "You make it sound as if the only thing that matters to me is roaming new pastures."

She blinked. He had expressed her feelings very well. And yet it seemed the idea was contemptuous to him.

"That isn't it at all." He pushed away from the wall. "Let me show you some of my work." He knelt before a stack. "This is some of my early work." He handed her a drawing and waited.

It was a simple sketch of a man hunched on a pile of boards, looking as if he had lost all hope.

"This is very good. It reminds me of the sketches you made at school, but it's much more"—she searched for the right word—"it says something."

His eyes took on a light. He handed her more—portraits of vacant-eyed men, drawings of men bent over a sluice box, pictures of men leering at a palmful of gold.

She had thought the photos of the Klondike were moving, but these sketches caught the stark emotions of individuals. "They're very powerful."

He moved to another stack. "These are paintings I made down the coastline." He picked out one and handed it to her. It showed ribbons of fog and a shadowy shoreline.

She touched it, almost expecting to feel moisture, and laughed a little. "It's so real." She let the painting pull at her senses until she breathed the damp air and felt the calmness of the drifting fog. "I like this."

"I have hundreds more sketches and paintings." He rose to his feet. "But there's something I especially want to show you." He moved to the table at the back of the room and pulled a worn leather portfolio toward him, then he untied the strings that held it closed. Then he seemed to think better of it and walked toward her, pausing a few feet away.

She wondered why he had changed his mind and watched him, mystified at the serious expression on his face and the way his eyes probed hers, searching for what she did not know.

"I guess most people think it was like a hike in the mountains to go looking for gold." He paused, his eyes still looking deep into hers until she felt he was seeing right into her soul. "It wasn't. All those who went fought a tough trail and discovered truths about themselves." He turned to look out the window. "Some found ugly, weak things. Others developed a strength beyond their imagination." Again he faced her. Again his eyes blazed into hers. "Many finally reached Dawson more broken than whole—more worn out than alive."

He rubbed the back of his neck. "It was like nothing I could describe. Men lined the streets, vacant eyed, empty. Mere shells. They seemed to have survived the trip but forgotten what life was about."

Sensing he was talking about something that had a profound effect on his life, Chas waited for him to continue.

He shifted and looked past her. "I guess I was one of those who having made the trip couldn't figure out what next. I wasn't interested in packing out to the gold camps. Gold wasn't the reason I had gone in the first place. Yet there seemed no place for me. I remember getting out my paper and pens and trying to draw, but I felt empty inside." He paced the room, as if he were experiencing again the emptiness he described.

"I remember walking along the river wanting to be by myself and figure out what I was going to do. I sat there for a long time, too weary and discouraged to move." He leaned against the wall, his look warm and knowing, as if he saw something in her she was unaware of. "I had taken my sketching materials with me."

Chas shifted her gaze away, but there was something compelling about his story—and the look in his eyes—that drew her despite her resolve.

He took a deep breath and continued. "I finally opened my materials and began leafing through them. I found a picture I had drawn long before I got there, while I was still in school. I looked at it for a long time while peace and purpose returned."

Chas felt caught like a moth before the lamplight, but after a second or two she managed to ask, "What was the picture?"

He smiled then, a smile so warm it made her blink.

"That's what I want to show you." He returned to the table and, flipping open the portfolio, picked up a tattered piece of paper and held it toward her.

She stepped forward and took it, wondering what had so inspired him. She saw the picture and gasped. "It's me." It was identical to the drawing he had done for her all those years ago. "I don't understand."

"Look at it again. What do you see?"

She examined it. "It's the same drawing you did for me that time I let you escape from Esther James."

"I made one for myself at the same time."

"I don't understand," she repeated, bending over again to study the picture, wistful pleasure tugging at her thoughts. "You have no idea how many times I looked at that picture wishing I could look like that."

It was his turn to look surprised. "That's how you do look."

She squinted at him. "Not now. Not ever. When you drew this, my hair was so flyaway it clung to my face and blew around my head like static. You've given me an expression that makes me look—"

"Serene, calm. And that's what you are and always were. I remember when the kids teased you about not having a father or living in a boardinghouse or even about your hair. You never let it upset you."

Chas laughed. "I told them I was special. My mother always told me I was and so surrounded me with love that I firmly believed it. When the kids teased me, I went inside myself to a place where I felt special and loved. Most days their teasing didn't bother me. I guess I was a solitary kid, but I was pretty happy most of the time."

For a heartbeat neither spoke. Chas tilted her head and studied Adam closely. "I still don't know why my picture would mean anything to you."

Shrugging, Adam looked past her. "I don't know if I can put it into words. Perhaps it was being reminded of your calmness." Embarrassed, he laughed a little. "All I can tell you is from that moment I knew I was going forward, and some-day I'd come back home." He shoved his hand through his hair. "As you can see, I almost wore the picture out." He crossed to a stack of paintings. "I decided I better replace it before it was worn to shreds." He turned a painting around for her to see.

Chas gasped as she stared at another likeness of herself, her flyaway fair hair spraying out around her head like a halo against the sky-blue background. Her eyes, which she consid-ered ordinary hazel, blazed a warm dark green. He had given her a shy half smile instead of the sober look of the sketch. She touched the painting, uncertain what to say.

He paced back and forth. "I returned to the hustling, dirty, crowded city."

She pulled her thoughts back to his story.

"I walked up and down the streets looking for something. I didn't know what, but I was sure I'd find it." He stopped in front of her and smiled. "And I did. I saw a man with his cam-era set up. For a price he was taking pictures of men to send back to their families or to keep for posterity. Even though most of them were broke and defeated, they wanted to prove they had made it.

"I watched for awhile. The photographer noticed my interest and called me over to help." Adam shrugged. "He taught me the whole business." He looked out the window. "And when he died a few months later, he left me all his equipment."

Adam fell silent for a moment and then walked to the desk and picked up the tattered sketch of Chas. "I carried this pic-ture of you in my heart all these years. I hoped you would still be here when I got back."

four

Chas's world tilted. She caught flashes of Adam's blue eyes as her gaze darted around the room. Finally she forced her frozen voice to speak. "I don't know what to say."

"You don't have to say anything. I just wanted to tell you."

He was smiling and relaxed.

She couldn't look directly at him.

One blaring question resounded in her brain. What did his confession mean?

She hurried toward the door, mumbling something about how much she'd enjoyed seeing his work, and stumbled outside. Emma would be wondering what was taking her so long, but Chas needed time to think, to let her tumbled thoughts settle. Her steps took her down the residential street, past the big turreted houses toward the white picket fence. As she passed, her eyes sought the arbor enclosing the table and chairs.

She choked back a sob. Her own father, Simon LaBlanc, had not cared enough to find out who she was. Yet a man she remembered only as a boy in school had carried her picture for ten years. *In his heart.*

She had told Adam she'd been raised to know she was special—a gift from God. But never had anything made her feel as special as this.

Later that evening, after her mother was settled and the house was quiet, Chas went to her little cubicle. It was barely big enough for her narrow bed, the tall wardrobe, and the tiny table she used for a desk; but it was her quiet haven. And how she needed to be alone and sort out her thoughts.

More than once after her return home, Emma had given her a strange look as she repeated a question Chas had missed.

"I get the feeling your mind is elsewhere." She had studied

Chas carefully. "Perhaps on a handsome man who has visited recently."

Chas pulled up short. "Adam?"

"Who else? Even Mrs. B, half blind as she is, finds him attractive."

Chas laughed. "I'm not denying he's handsome."

"Nobody would believe you if you did." Emma bent over the pot of potatoes and leaned on the masher. "Don't forget he's also charming, considerate, and interesting."

Chas stirred the gravy. "And as likely to settle down in one place as I am to fly."

Emma straightened to look at her. "What's so wrong with a little adventure in your life?"

"I'm not opposed to adventure," Chas protested, trying to marshall her thoughts. "It makes life interesting and fun. But I think we need to be careful of the risks involved." She paused, wondering how to explain. "Take my mother, for instance. She thought she had found a handsome, charming man and decided it would be fun to join his adventure of moving West. Look where it got her."

Emma's eyes narrowed. "Seems to me she's happy enough with where it got her. She has this boardinghouse and you. I've never heard her complain. Not once."

"You're right, of course. God turned her mistakes into good. But that doesn't mean it's a good idea to rush headlong into things and hope God will send an angel to rescue you."

"You make it sound as if you expect Adam to rush off to the North Pole for a dozen years or more."

Chas shrugged. "Maybe. After all, he took ten years to go to the Yukon."

"Yes, but what better time to wander free than as a young man with no responsibilities." Emma dished the potatoes into a large bowl. "I guess he's decided it's time to settle down."

"I doubt it, but it's neither here nor there to me."

Emma let out her breath. "You're already half in love with him. Not that I blame you."

Chas almost dropped the platter of meat. "Emma, I am not. When I fall in love and marry, it will be with someone I know will always be there."

Emma nodded. "Someone dull and steady and as predictable as the rising of the sun. Michael, I suppose."

"There's nothing wrong with Michael. He's not dull. He's comfortable and a good friend. Being content to stay in one place doesn't mean you have to be dull."

Emma had waited until she was halfway through the door to the dining room to mumble, "Maybe Michael's an exception then."

Now, in the sanctuary of her room, the troubling emotions of the day swept over Chas.

She hurried to the little table and sat down, pulling out a sheet of paper and dipping her pen in the ink. She wrote in neat letters across the top of the page: Simon LaBlanc. It was all she knew of her father. Her mother's parents had been dead many years before she married Simon LaBlanc, but Chas wondered if either of his parents was still alive. Could she have grandparents somewhere, perhaps the grandmother from whom she had inherited her fair coloring?

She sighed. They wouldn't even know she existed.

She ran her fingers back and forth across the letters of his name. He could be, and probably was, the worst sort of scoundrel; yet there was something comforting in knowing his name. Finally she folded the paper in half and slipped it between the pages of her Bible.

She dragged her chair to the wardrobe and reached to the far corner of the top shelf for a box. She carried it to the table and untied the strings. Inside was an assortment of essays and graded papers. About halfway down she found what she was looking for—a piece of heavier, grainier paper—and pulled it out. It was the drawing Adam had made of her. She stared at herself for several seconds and then carried it to the mirror on the door of the wardrobe and held it next to her face.

She looked from her own image to the reflection of the

drawing, trying to see why Adam had found encouragement in remembering her. Had she even thought of Adam in the last ten years? Of course she had wondered at first, like everyone else, how he could leave like that and how long he would be gone. Then she'd forgotten him, except for the occasional reminder when Mrs. Silverhorn mentioned she had received a letter.

Yet he had thought of her all that time.

He had carried her in his heart.

The words fluttered through her along with Emma's announcement: "I think you're already half in love with him." Emma had also warned Chas that falling in love with Adam would mean excitement and adventure.

Chas shook her head. She wasn't opposed to a bit of excitement, but neither was she willing to risk losing the sort of life she had always dreamed of.

She pushed the drawing back in the box, retied the strings, and returned the box to the top shelf.

Falling in love with Adam was out of the question. It simply did not fit in with what she wanted for her life.

She opened her Bible and read a little, then bowed to pray, promising God she would trust Him to guide her future and asking for strength to serve Him in her current situation.

And keep me from foolishness, she prayed, thinking how handsome Adam looked and how her heart had almost exploded when he said he'd carried her picture in his heart.

❧

Tea was over. Mr. Elias had gone for his walk. Mother sat in the front room helping Mrs. B with her doily.

Emma pulled the roaster out of the oven. "I'll check the meat. Then I guess everything is ready. Looks as if we'll have a few minutes to spare today."

Chas poured a cup of tea. "I'm going to take this out to the veranda. Join me when you're finished."

Emma nodded in agreement as Chas stepped out the back door to one of her favorite spots, the bench at the end of the veranda. A latticed wall provided a feeling of privacy without shutting out the view.

She had taken a book with her and opened its pages. After a few minutes she discovered she was restless and unable to concentrate and laid it aside.

"Hello, Miss LaBlanc."

She lifted her gaze to the sound and met three pairs of eyes over the gate at the bottom of the garden and grinned at the wide-eyed look they each gave her.

Jack, Adam's younger brother, had greeted her. She addressed him first. "Hello, Jack." Then she turned to Adam and his sister. "Hello, Ellen and Adam. How are you?"

"We're fine," Jack answered for all three. "We're just out for a walk."

"Would you like to come in?"

Adam opened the gate before she finished asking, and the three trooped up the walk to the veranda. There weren't enough chairs, but Adam perched on the railing as Ellen sat in the wooden chair facing Chas.

Jack plopped down on the veranda floor. "Adam says we deserve a break because we've been working so hard. We got a lot done, didn't we, Adam?"

Adam ruffled the boy's hair and grinned at him. "We surely did." His gaze sought Chas's eyes. "We put up the backdrops for portraits, and then we set up the first display of pictures."

"First display?" Chas said.

"I have far too many photos and pictures to hang at once, so I plan to change them every month or two."

"We did the Klondike this time," Jack added. "But we only used the pictures that showed a broad view of the area."

Chas knew he was quoting Adam.

"I thought he should have shown all those gold rush pictures."

Adam chuckled. "Maybe another time, Youngster."

Chas turned to include Ellen in the conversation and caught the adoring look she gave her older brother. "What did he have you doing, Ellen?"

The girl lowered her head, hiding her face, and mumbled,

"I helped him pick out the pictures to hang."

Remembering the stacks of pictures, Chas shook her head. "It must have been difficult to choose."

Ellen looked up at Chas. "I wanted to show just paintings, but he said I had to choose photos and sketches as well. His paintings are so wonderful." The girl's voice was filled with admiration.

"Ellen could be a bit prejudiced in her judgment," Adam said with a drawl.

Ellen spun on him. "Am not. Your paintings are good. You should be proud of yourself."

Chas drew in her breath, waiting for Adam's reply.

He leaned back, his legs crossed at the ankles, his hands resting on the ledge, smiling down at Ellen with an expression that caused Chas's throat to tighten. "I'm happy with my work. It gives me pleasure. But there's room for improvement."

"How can you say that?" Ellen demanded.

Adam shrugged. "There's always room for improvement. If I as an artist, or anyone else for that matter, sit back and accept things as being as good as they'll get, there would be little progress made in this world."

Ellen drew back. "Well, I think your paintings are perfect."

Adam gave a low chuckle. "Ellen, thank you for your loyalty."

Jack suddenly sat up and leaned toward Chas. "We came to invite you to see the display. It'll be ready Monday, won't it, Adam?"

Adam nodded.

Jack rushed on. "Tomorrow Adam is taking us to Sheep Falls. Have you ever been there, Miss LaBlanc?"

Chas shook her head. "I hear it's lovely."

"You should come with us."

Adam leaned forward. "Good idea, Jack."

"Yes, do," added Ellen.

Chas looked from Jack with his eager face, to Ellen smiling shyly, to Adam. At his dark searching look, her heart stalled.

"What about it, Chas?" he asked.

Her gaze darted away and then returned to Adam's eyes. Just as quickly, she pulled away again, unable to deal with what she saw there. "I couldn't," she murmured, choosing to study her fingers. "I have my work."

"Couldn't Emma manage for a day?" Adam asked, his low voice pleading gently.

"I couldn't ask her."

The back door squealed, then slapped shut, and Emma joined them. "Why is everyone looking at me?" she demanded.

Jack scooted forward to face her. "We want Miss LaBlanc to go with us tomorrow."

"Adam's taking us to the falls," Ellen added.

"But she doesn't think she can leave for the day," said Adam.

Emma laughed. "And you want me to persuade her it's all right to go and let me run things for the day?"

Three heads bobbed up and down.

"It's fine with me." She turned to Chas. "I can manage. You run along and enjoy yourself."

Chas scowled at the knowing grin on Emma's face and the slight emphasis she put on the word "enjoy."

"It's settled then," Adam said, leaning back.

"Yeah!" Jack yelled.

Ellen suddenly lost her restraint. "We'll have a lovely time."

ミ

It was late before Chas got to bed.

Sunday was traditionally a day of rest with cold meals, which meant preparing twice as much food on Saturday. Chas felt guilty leaving Emma with the extra work, so she had cooked potatoes and boiled eggs and diced them for potato salad. While the potatoes cooked, she had baked several cakes. Emma would cook the turkey and serve it hot Saturday, slicing the rest for Sunday's cold dinner.

Although pleasantly tired, Chas didn't go to sleep at once. Butterflies fluttered in her stomach.

She looked forward to seeing the falls—the local attraction.

But, forcing herself to be honest, she admitted she was also deeply curious about the man who said he had thought of her all those years.

ஓ

The sky shone like a mirror as they made the two-hour journey to the falls.

"It's a perfect day," Ellen said from her seat behind Chas.

"Couldn't ask for better," agreed Adam, glancing at Chas.

She suddenly found the passing scenery required her full attention. During the night she had decided to forget he'd thought of her for the past ten years; it was simply some romantic notion born of loneliness and desperation. She would treat him as an old friend, nothing more. But the way his eyes continually sought her, at once compelling and proprietorial, made it difficult to remember her decision.

"Makes me feel like singing." And to prove her point, Ellen started: "Oh, my darling, oh, my darling, oh, my darling Clementine."

Glad of the diversion, Chas relaxed.

Ellen had a sweet, clear voice, and the others listened as she sang the first verse. As she started the chorus again, Jack's uncertain voice joined hers.

Adam smiled over his shoulder and then joined his siblings, his deeper voice rounding out the trio. They finished the song and laughed together.

Chas sat back, watching Adam with his younger brother and sister, enjoying the way he was at ease with them.

Ellen started another song.

"Come on, Chas." Adam smiled at her. "Sing with us."

She couldn't resist the twinkling challenge in his eyes, feeling all the while she was being sucked further and further from her decision.

They sang song after song.

Ellen and Jack taught them some new choruses they had learned at school.

"Remember this one?" Adam grinned at Chas and began a

song they had learned in school.

"Where did you hear that?" Jack asked.

"At school." His warm eyes lingered on Chas's face.

"It must be really old."

Both Chas and Adam laughed. Then Adam reached back to squeeze Jack's knee.

"Are you calling me an old man?"

Jack grabbed Adam's arm and pretended to twist it up behind the seat. "You're pretty old all right."

Adam turned around and half lifted Jack from his seat. "Not too old to handle you, Sprout."

Jack clung to Adam's fist, giggling. "I'll grow up soon enough, and by then you'll be really old."

Chas watched the interplay, knowing Adam had already earned the innocent love of both his sister and brother, and she envied their mutual affection. Life as an only child had often left her wishing for a brother or sister, or both, to share secrets with or simply to enjoy the sort of play she saw here.

They edged down a narrow trail through the trees. Adam pulled the horses to a stop.

"Listen. Hear it?"

Chas tilted her head, catching the rumble of the falls. She leaned forward, straining for her first glimpse.

"Relax. It's still a distance before you can see it."

Jack bounced on the seat, rocking the buggy. "Hurry up, Adam."

Chuckling, Adam flicked the reins, and they rattled forward.

Suddenly sunlight flashed on the water, momentarily blinding Chas. Then she saw the falls, a mane of white water tumbling from the rocks above, crashing to the foaming cauldron before them. Chas tasted the cool mist on her lips. The roar drowned out all other sound.

Adam leaned close and yelled in her ear, "We're here!"

It was such an unnecessary bit of information that she shouted with soundless laughter.

"I noticed!" she exclaimed, grinning back.

He shook his head, indicating he couldn't hear, and leaned close. A whiff of spicy shaving soap drifted across her senses. She tasted the moisture on her lips again and tried to satisfy her lungs with the damp air.

"You'll have to yell in my ear," he roared, his breath teasing her hair, warming her cheek, making her acutely aware of his nearness.

Determined to remain unaffected, she nodded and turned to shout in his ear, instead staring into his eyes, the sunlight reflected in his irises. His eyes invited her—she swallowed hard—to what she couldn't say. But she knew the invitation carried with it risks she vowed she would not take.

She shook her head, indicating she didn't wish to repeat her statement, and sat back, her gaze on the falls.

The buggy bounced as Ellen and Jack jumped down.

Chas stared at them and then turned to Adam. "What—?"

Remembering he couldn't hear, she raised her eyebrows, silently asking what they were doing.

Adam draped the reins and jumped down, coming to her side to hold out a hand. Curiosity overcoming caution, Chas allowed him to help her down and lead her to the edge of the rocks where the spray washed their skin.

Chas couldn't take her eyes off the boiling water. It was like standing in the pit of a storm.

She had almost forgotten the rest of them until Adam touched her shoulder. She started at his touch. He tilted his head toward the hill where Jack was scrambling up a narrow trail and Ellen was clutching at the bushes as she followed him.

Adam held out his hand. Surrounded by the deep-throated roar of the falls, she allowed him to take her hand and lead her up the path. Diamonds dripped from every leaf and clung to every blade of grass. A rainbow caught in the mist, and she pointed to it.

Adam nodded, then flashed a smile at her, mouthing words she couldn't hear. Shrugging, she took another step up the trail. Adam didn't move. On the narrow path their shoulders touched, their still-clasped hands brushed her leg.

Moisture beaded on his lashes. One silvery drop splashed on his cheek. In the mist-shrouded scene, his blue eyes were warm and intense.

She welcomed the cool moisture and tore her gaze away, seeking the rising trail. He led the way, and she could finally fill her lungs with the heavy moisture-laden air.

As they climbed, the noise of the water softened to a murmur. They struggled over a rocky bench and stepped into a wide, grassy meadow. The river here was wide and quiet.

Ellen sat close to the bank, tossing bits of grass into the water.

Jack explored the underbrush of the trees.

Chas dropped Adam's hand and stepped away. Welcoming the warmth after the dampness of the trail, she turned her face to the sun rather than meet Adam's eyes.

But she could not avoid him forever. Slowly she forced herself to turn. But he was gone. She turned full circle, wondering if he had joined Jack or Ellen, but he wasn't with them. She shrugged. But it was disappointment rather than relief she felt as she ambled to Ellen's side and dropped down on the grass beside her.

"It's so beautiful here," Ellen murmured. "I wish we could stay here forever, just Adam and us."

"You're really enjoying having him home, aren't you?"

Ellen beamed. "Oh, yes, it's wonderful."

The girl's words troubled Chas, but how could she warn Ellen her brother was only looking for a home base?

Ellen glanced over her shoulder. "Where's Adam?"

"I don't know."

"Here I am." Breathing hard, Adam stood at the top of the trail. "I went back to get my sketchbook." He held out a large black-covered book. "Too many good things to waste." He sat on a rock several feet away, his pencil already busy.

He occasionally glanced toward Chas and Ellen, but every time Chas looked, he had his attention on the page. She tried to forget he was there.

Jack bounded to Adam's side, peering over his shoulder. "Hey, that's pretty good."

"Thanks, Sprout. What have you been up to?"

Jack shrugged. "Just looking around." He shoved his hands in his pockets and rocked back on his heels.

Recognizing his stance as an imitation of Adam, Chas lowered her head to hide a smile.

"I'm hungry," he announced.

Adam closed the sketchbook. "Me too. Come on, Girls. Let's go back."

Chas jumped to her feet, brushing her skirt with her hand. Jack was already leaping over the rocks.

"Jack, slow down," Adam cautioned. "I wouldn't want to have to fish you out of the water."

"Okay!" Jack called out, leaping over another rock.

Adam stood back, waiting for Ellen to follow her younger brother.

"Are you enjoying yourself?" he asked Chas, falling into step at her side.

"It's lovely," she murmured, keeping her attention on the path. The rocks proved difficult to traverse, and she admired Jack's nimbleness in jumping over them. Her foot slipped. She grabbed at a bush to steady herself and found instead a warm hand.

"Better let me help," he said. "Wouldn't want to fish you out of the water either."

His touch did more to her than steady her steps—much more. Things she didn't want; things she had promised wouldn't happen. But the trail was steep and slippery, and she welcomed his help, while remaining vexed at the waywardness of her heart.

She blinked the mist from her eyes. He would be gone as suddenly as he had returned. A man with no roots. Her resolve returned, strong enough to enable her to cling to his hand without letting her emotions dissolve into a vapor.

The roar of the water made conversation impossible,

allowing her to concentrate on the trail as she scolded herself mentally.

They stepped to level ground, and she pulled away from his grip, clutching her fingers together to prove her inner victory.

Ellen and Jack were already seated in the buggy.

Chas hurried over, but before she could step up on her own, Adam was at her side taking her hand. She nodded her thanks without meeting his eyes. She felt his surprise when she busied herself smoothing her skirt rather than looking at him.

Slowly he released her hand.

She drew a shaky breath. *Please, God, give me strength to be true to my convictions.*

They drove along the river's edge to a clearing where they spread blankets. Ellen opened the large basket and began to set out the food.

As they ate, Chas turned to Jack. "How is school going?"

"Okay," he mumbled, his eyes downcast.

When he didn't say anything more, she prodded. "Jack, is there a problem?" She had always found him an eager student.

He shrugged. "It's just I don't like Mr. Martin as much as you."

"Why, thank you, Jack." She thought the children would have forgotten her.

"You said you'd come back."

She had explained to her class that she had to leave to take care of her mother, but she thought then it would be only a month or two. "I know I did—and I want to. But, you see, my mother still can't manage on her own. She needs me."

A thoughtful look crossed his face for a moment. "Yep," he finally said, "if someone you love needs you, you should look after them."

"I agree." She didn't dare look at Adam. She was afraid for all of them—Jack, Ellen, herself. What would happen to them when Adam left again?

Ellen asked, "You won't leave again, will you, Adam?"

Chas caught her breath, waiting for his reply.

"I can't promise I won't go see what's going on in another part of the country. But I can promise you I'll always come back."

Ellen lowered her head, but not before Chas glimpsed her look of disappointment. He didn't say when he'd come back. Ten years maybe? She twisted a blade of grass around her finger. A person would never be certain with Adam.

Jack sprang to his feet. "Can I go wading, Adam?"

"I don't see why not."

"Thanks." Jack sprinted to the river.

"Take off your shoes and socks and roll up your pants first."

Jack shot an adults-are-so-strange look over his shoulder. "As if I'd forget."

Adam laughed. "It's happened before."

Ellen tugged on Chas's hand. "Let's go."

She followed Ellen behind some bushes, where they took off their shoes and stockings.

She dipped a foot in the cold water and hesitated, but Ellen raced in splashing and squealing.

She wondered if Adam would join them, but he sat on the bank, sketchbook on his knee. She felt awkward and not a little immature at his amused expression.

"Come on, Adam!" Jack called. "It's fun."

"I'll just watch."

"Aw, come on." Jack scooped up a handful of water and threw it at him.

Adam ducked and rolled away.

Laughing, Jack threw more water.

Adam tossed a handful of pebbles into the water in front of Jack, but the splash posed no threat to the boy.

Jack paddled his hands in the water, trying to soak Adam, and succeeded in drenching himself.

Adam retreated along the shore with Jack in pursuit.

"Enough," Adam ordered.

And Jack quit, more so, Chas was sure, because he was

laughing too hard to continue than because he felt like obeying. He plowed through the water toward the girls, with Adam following more sedately at a safe distance.

Ellen trailed her fingers through the water, singing softly.

"Stop."

At Adam's sharp word, everyone froze.

"Don't move," Adam ordered.

"What's the matter?" Afraid to breathe lest she invite some lurking danger, Chas kept her eyes on Adam's face.

A slow smile widened his mouth. "Stay right where you are."

She moved nothing but her eyes. "Jack?"

His eyes were saucers.

"Don't move," Adam said again, grabbing his sketchbook. "The sun has caught the moisture around your head. It looks as if you're wearing a rainbow halo."

Chas forced herself to stand still, though she inwardly squirmed at the way Adam stared, then looked down to draw a few lines.

After a moment he lowered the paper. "It's gone."

She longed to see what he had drawn, but his bright-eyed intensity made her keep quiet.

The cold seeped upward from her ankles, and, shivering, she hurried from the water.

"You were so pretty, Miss LaBlanc," Jack said, his voice squeaky.

Grateful for a reason to flee Adam's look, Chas ducked behind the bushes to pull on her stockings and shoes.

When she returned, Adam lounged against a tree, his sketch pad at his side. She chose a spot within easy talking distance but far enough away to give her some confidence.

Jack pulled himself from the water, soaked from head to toe. "Let's go exploring," he said to Adam.

Adam rested his head against the tree. "You go ahead, Sprout. I think I'll stay right here."

Jack called over his shoulder, "Come on, Ellen. Let's go."

His sister hurried to put on her stockings and shoes, and the two set off. Chas wavered, not knowing if she should follow them or stay where she was.

"Chas and I will stay here," Adam told the others, settling the question.

Adam lay back, and Chas relaxed, enjoying the murmur of the water, the chatter of birds, the fresh pine scent. The sun was warm, and she let her tension seep away.

She had almost dozed off when Adam stirred, rustling the pine needles. She kept her eyes closed, not wanting to end the delicious sense of peace, but she could hear him turning the pages of his sketchbook.

He cleared his throat. "I thought you might like to see the sketch I did."

She sat up. "I would indeed."

He scooted over, laying the open book on her knees. She saw herself, face framed by spray, hair tossed up. She looked so ordinary.

"It's just a crude sketch," Adam murmured in her ear. "You can't see how the light broke into a full spectrum around your head. It was really quite unusual."

"I wish I could have seen it."

He chuckled. "Wait until I paint it—that is, if you'll give your permission?"

There seemed no reason to refuse. "What would you do with it?"

"Guess it depends on what you want. You could have it if you like, or I could add it to my collection." He hesitated. "I would love to do that."

Confused, she asked, "Do what? Paint the picture or add it to your collection?"

"Both."

He flipped a page. She and Ellen sat at the riverbank. He flipped another page, and she laughed at the drawing of Jack jumping in the water, his mischievousness captured perfectly.

Adam showed her several more sketches and then, leaning back on his elbows, looked at her.

She tried not to let her gaze jump about. Finally she demanded, "Why are you staring at me?"

He pulled his gaze away. "I'm sorry. I didn't realize I was."

She didn't speak.

"I had to come back," he offered.

She nodded. "I know a young boy and girl who are grateful you did."

"I suppose they're the only ones?"

Aware he was watching her closely, she made a great study of the pinecone she had plucked off the ground. "I'm sure a mother and father are equally grateful."

"Hmm. Anyone else?"

She looked down the trail. "You don't suppose they've encountered a problem, do you?"

"I'm sure they're fine."

She sighed, looking everywhere but at Adam. "This is a really lovely place. I'm glad Jack invited me along."

"I had to see if you were as I remembered."

It still amazed her he claimed to remember so much of her. She faced him, instantly regretting her action as his blue gaze caught and held her like a trap.

"I thought I might have actually created you in my imagination." The pulse in his throat beat with steady rhythm, echoing in her emotions. "I was in love with a memory and had to find out if it was real."

She jolted to her feet, half running down the path in pursuit of Ellen and Jack. "I think we should check on them," she called, not caring if he thought she was acting strangely. She couldn't bear to hear any more.

Emma's words rang in her ears: "Don't go falling in love with him." She had promised she wouldn't, thinking it would be easy. He was just the opposite of what she wanted.

She tried to calm her pounding thoughts. She knew what she wanted. Someone steady, someone she could count on. Someone like Michael. Her insides settled.

Yes, Michael was exactly what she needed.

five

She caught up to Jack and Ellen and called them to return.

On the way back, Jack poked into every tree stump while Ellen picked flowers. Chas followed slowly, welcoming the chance to settle her thoughts before she had to face Adam again.

When they marched into the clearing, Adam was intent on his sketchbook. He stood and stretched. "Good. You're back. It's time we headed home."

"Aww," Jack began, "already?"

Adam ruffled Jack's hair. "I promised Chas I'd have her back for supper." He scooped up his drawing materials and started toward the buggy.

Jack blocked Chas's path. "Couldn't we stay longer?" he begged.

Chas smiled down at the boy. "I'm sorry, Jack, but I promised Emma I'd be back."

"Couldn't you break your promise?"

"No, Jack, I wouldn't do that."

The boy studied her for another moment. "It wouldn't be honest, would it?"

"No, it wouldn't be. People should be able to trust what we say."

"Come on, Sprout." Adam stood beside the buggy.

Jack nodded thoughtfully before he sprinted toward Adam.

Chas would have preferred to climb up on her own, but Adam waited, hands planted on his hips, leaving her no choice but to go to his side. Grabbing a deep breath, she reached for the hand he extended, keeping her eyes on the step. He released her hand quickly, turning to help Ellen.

Chas clutched her hands together in her lap, staring ahead

as Adam took his seat and flicked the reins.

He didn't speak until they were away from the noise of the falls. "Did everyone have a good time?"

Two voices from the backseat chorused, "Yes."

"Thank you, Adam." Chas angled a glance at him.

He smiled. "My pleasure." His silver-threaded gaze returned to the trail.

At his impersonal response, Chas wondered if she had imagined the passion of his earlier confession. But the way he had looked at her—seeking—insisting—on a response she didn't feel able to give, had not been a fancy of her wayward thoughts. It had been there. It had been real.

The homeward journey was quiet. The two in the backseat, Chas suspected, were tired. She was content in her own thoughts, as long as she avoided remembering Adam's behavior at the river.

In front of the boardinghouse, Adam reached behind the seat to grab his drawing pad and pulled out two pages. "I want you to have these. To remember your first trip to the falls."

One sketch was of the falls. Even on paper, the water appeared to roll and churn. The other was of Chas and Ellen splashing in the river, their skirts tucked up to their knees. Ellen was attempting to catch a drop of water; Chas appeared fascinated with the splash her feet made.

A lump swelled in her throat at Adam's kindness, and she allowed herself to look at him. "It was a wonderful day, Adam. I'll cherish it always."

The taut lines around his mouth disappeared as he smiled. "Me too."

She turned to bid good-bye to the others.

"Don't forget to come to Adam's shop on Monday," Jack reminded her.

"I won't," she said.

She stepped away from the buggy, waving good-bye to them, and barely had time to turn toward the house before Emma yanked open the door. "So? How was your date?"

Chas rolled her eyes. "It was an outing, not a date."

Emma tossed her head. "And I'm a chef, not a cook."

"Have you been to the falls?"

"A teacher took us once several years ago." She planted herself in front of Chas. "I don't want to know about the falls. I want to know about Adam."

Chas wrinkled her nose. "Then maybe you should have gone with him."

Emma waved her hand in dismissal. "I don't mean for me, Silly. How did Adam treat you?"

"Like a gentleman, of course."

Emma stalked to the stove, checking to see if the kettle had boiled. "You are so dense sometimes."

Chas looked down. She knew what Emma was getting at, but she didn't want to think about it. His devotion to her memory made her uncomfortable. The sketches in her hand provided the perfect escape. "Here—look at these."

Emma snatched them from her hand, looking at one and then the other, then tossing them on the table. "So you played in the water with Ellen."

Chas chuckled. "What did you expect?" Before Emma could answer, she hurried on. "How was Mother?"

Emma lifted her shoulders in a deep sigh. "She's fine. Helped me ice the cakes and mix the potato salad."

Chas opened her mouth to protest, but Emma lifted a hand to stop her. "I put everything on the table within reach. Chas, she needs to know she's needed and that we appreciate her help."

Chas nodded. "But every time I allow her to do something, she overdoes it."

"I know. But she's learned her lesson. All she wants to do now is get better. I'm sure she'll do whatever she must."

"She said all that?"

Emma shrugged. "Sort of."

"Where is she now?"

Emma pressed her hand to her mouth. "Whoops. I forgot to

tell you Michael is here already. She's visiting with him in the sitting room."

Chas groaned. She wanted to change her clothes and wash off the sand and dust. Then the meal needed to be prepared. "What still needs to be done?"

"Everything's ready and keeping warm in the oven. I just have to make the tea and put out the food."

"Give me a minute to change. I'll let Mother and Michael know I'm home. Then I'll give you a hand." She paused at the door. "Didn't you have plans for tonight?"

Emma nodded. "Pastor Simpson and Miss Martha have invited half a dozen of us over to meet a cousin of theirs or something." She wrinkled her nose. "Probably some old codger, but I promised Dorothy I'd go with her."

Chas nodded. "There's no need for you to stay. Run along and enjoy your evening."

Emma shook her head. "I have lots of time. I'll help clean up the meal before I leave."

"Emma, you're a gem. I don't know what I'd do without you."

Emma gave her a mischievous look. "You could ask Stella back."

Remembering those first days of Stella's criticism and refusal to accept Chas's authority, Chas shuddered. "I'm grateful to say she would never consider it." She hurried down the hall. "I'll be right back."

A few minutes later everything was served. Beryl and Louise were out, having gone with their beaus; the Knutsen boys had left after work for a visit to the farm; and John was absent. But the rest settled around the table.

Mrs. B leaned over to Mother. "Your girl is back. Where did you say she was?"

"She went to Sheep Falls!" the younger woman yelled close to Mrs. B's ear.

Mrs. B looked annoyed. "What does she want with balls?"

"Not balls, Sheep Falls."

"What difference does it make if they are cheap?" She shook her head. "You better keep an eye on her, Marie." She unfolded her napkin on her lap and sat up straight, waiting for a signal to begin eating.

Mother laughed, winking at Chas. "I do my best, Ida." But everyone knew the comment was not for Mrs. B's ears. "Now let's pray." She took Chas's hand, giving it a little squeeze, taking away any sting Mrs. B's words might have carried.

Chas bowed her head, silently thanking God for His bountiful provision, adding a special thanks for her dear mother who made life special.

Mother murmured, "Amen."

For several minutes conversation was confined to getting the food passed around the table. When the bowls and platters had circled the table, Roy leaned around Michael.

"Were you able to estimate the height of the falls?"

Chas shook her head. "No, Roy, but we did climb to the top of them."

"Did it take long?"

"It didn't seem long. I guess I never paid it much mind."

Emma grinned. "She had other things on her mind."

Michael stiffened, and Chas glowered at Emma.

Mr. Elias leaned forward. "I expect Adam could answer your questions, Roy. He's a knowledgeable young man with a head for learning."

Satisfied, Roy leaned back. "Yes, I'll ask him." He glanced at Chas. "Though I can't understand how someone could go there and not notice anything about it."

Chas laughed out loud. "I noticed lots of things, Roy. I just didn't measure anything."

"It's all the same," Roy said, frowning. "Isn't it?"

Still smiling, Chas shook her head. "Not necessarily. For instance, I noticed how the mist from the falls made rainbows over the water. I noticed the way the flowers and vines clung to the wet rocks. I saw how the tumbling water churned around the rocks in a magical dance."

"How much water do you think flows over every minute?"

Chuckling, Chas shook her head. "I have no idea. How would one even measure it?"

Roy grew thoughtful. "You could set up—"

Emma put her fork down and wrinkled her nose at Roy. "How would you expect her to care about scientific nonsense when she was with Adam? I tell you, I would have had my eyes on nothing else. Not even trees and flowers."

Chas glared at Emma, silently warning her to stop.

"Now there's a young man with a bright future." Mr. Elias announced. "I assure you he will go a long way."

Michael held his fork halfway to his mouth and said, "Seems he's gone a long way already. The Yukon, Alaska—where else did he say he went?"

Roy supplied the answer. "He made the thousand-mile trip down the inside passage and then explored the islands of the passage."

"Thank you, Roy," Emma said. "I'm guessing he was more interested in the people and scenery than in how far it was from point A to point B."

Roy drew back. "He's the one who told me this."

Chas jumped up. "He did a couple of sketches at the falls. I'll get them." She hurried to the kitchen to retrieve them, handing them to her mother to pass around.

Mrs. B bent close to the one with Chas in it. "Isn't this Chastity?" She looked across at Chas as if she expected her to have sprouted a second head.

"She went there this morning!" Mother shouted.

"I know she wasn't here this morning. She was out playing ball." Mrs. B looked at the picture again. "Who are these girls playing in the water?"

Rather than try to make her understand, Mother handed her the other sketch. "Sheep Falls," she yelled, pointing to the words Adam had penciled at the bottom of the page.

Mrs. B studied the picture without comment before she handed it on.

"He's a good artist," Emma said, handing the pages on to Mr. Elias.

The pictures went around the table with no one arguing the point. Shortly afterward, the residents began to push away from the table. It didn't take long to clean up, and Emma was soon on her way.

Chas returned to the living room, where Michael sat visiting with Roy.

"Let's go out on the veranda," she suggested.

"Good idea." Michael sprang to his feet.

The cool night air held a hint of moisture, taking her, despite herself, to thoughts of the afternoon spent at the falls. Deftly she pulled her thoughts away, resting them instead on the man beside her on the bench. "It's a lovely evening."

"I guess sitting out here is rather dull after your outing this afternoon." His voice was mournful.

"Oh, no. It's peaceful and calm, and I like that. Besides, it's far from dull. Look at the way the moon glistens off the leaves. What more could I ask for than to sit on my own back step and enjoy the evening?"

He shifted about. "I've never taken you anywhere special." He cleared his throat. "I always thought you were content right here."

She grabbed at his arm, anxious to clear up this misunderstanding. "I always have been. I still am. I've never hankered after excitement." She wanted to tell him not to worry. The one thing she always enjoyed about her friendship with Michael was how comfortable they were together. *Not like Adam.* She jerked her thoughts back. He shouldn't have bothered to come back. All he'd done was disrupt her life. She wouldn't think of him anymore. Not with Michael beside her wondering if he had failed.

"He's full of adventure," Michael said, "and tales of faraway places."

"Yes, he is. He has wonderful stories."

"And he's very artistic."

"Yes, he's that too." It felt like an argument with herself. He was all of these things, but— "I'm not looking for instability."

"I suppose he'll be around just long enough to turn everything upside down, and then he'll leave."

It was an echo of her own sentiments. "Some people prefer the predictable, the conventional."

"Put that way, it sounds deadly dull."

She squeezed his arm. "I don't mean dull. I mean stable and secure—knowing the one you love will walk through the door every day and sit across the table from you each meal. And be there every morning, every night. Go to church with you every Sunday."

At first, Michael didn't answer. Then he covered her hand with his own. "Have you fallen in love with Adam?"

She jumped to her feet, facing him in the cold moonlight. "Didn't you hear a word I said? He's not my sort. I don't want the kind of life he'd want. I want a home and stability. I want—" Breathless, she broke off and dropped down beside him again, her voice falling to a whisper. "I want a real home, a real family. I don't want to end up like Mother, alone in a big house that isn't even a home."

He took her hand and tucked it around his arm, holding her close to his side, and she relaxed, content to enjoy the comfort of his presence.

After some moments he broke the peaceful silence between them. "I'm not arguing with you, but I don't think you need to feel sorry about how your mother's lived her life. She seems very happy with her lot."

"I know. But I've always dreamed of more." In her mind she stood at the white picket fence looking at the little house and its pleasant yard. She laughed a little at the comparison. "Maybe I should say I've dreamed of something less—a little house of my own rather than the boardinghouse."

She could feel Michael nod. "Maybe it's time to think about fulfilling some of those dreams." His hand tightened around hers.

She held her breath.

"I always hoped we'd become more than friends." His warm breath flitted across her cheek, sending little thrills up and down her spine.

She pulled in air, forcing it down into her lungs, telling herself to be calm. "You never said anything." She didn't succeed in keeping the quiver from her voice.

He lifted their clasped hands a few inches. "I figured we'd grow close at our own rate."

She wondered how long it would have taken for him to announce all this without Adam's arrival to speed him up. Another two years? Then, shamed at her unkindness, she squeezed his hand. "That's so thoughtful."

"I believe in caution when it comes to relationships. They so often turn out to be something other than what we first thought."

She sat back a little. His words sounded like a warning. Or perhaps bitter experience. Suddenly she realized how little she knew of him, considering the length of time they had known one another.

"Did you have a relationship that went bad?" The words stuck in her throat, but she needed to understand him better.

He stiffened, almost pulling his hand away, and then, changing his mind, squeezed her fingers. "I was speaking generally. When we're young we approach all relationships with a wide-eyed trust. Time teaches us to be more selective."

He had avoided her question. The fact that he chose not to answer directly bothered her. She wanted him to trust her enough to be open and honest.

"I think there's more to it than you're admitting." Her voice was low, her words gentle. Despite her desire for honesty between them, she didn't want to force him into a discussion he wished to avoid. "But I know you'll discuss it when you feel the time is right."

Minutes passed. The pale moonlight cast gray shadows across the yard, ghostly suggestions of trees and objects. A cat howled. Somewhere a dog barked, the mournful sound echoing in her soul.

"I did have a bad experience," Michael offered, his voice slow and silvery in the quiet. "I thought we had an understanding, but Miriam thought differently. She walked away without so much as a good-bye."

She squeezed his hand. "Michael, I'm so sorry."

"I got over it. I guess in a way I wasn't all that surprised."

"Why didn't it surprise you?"

He drew in a breath. "My parents never cared for me as much as my brother. I guess I didn't expect she would be any different."

She gasped. "Miriam ran off with Timothy?"

"That would have been poetic justice, don't you think?" His laugh was short and bitter. "No, it was someone else. But I guess it proved to me no one would ever care for me enough to love me unconditionally." His fingers tightened around her hand. "But in all the time I've known you, you have always been honest and true."

"Thank you, Michael." A sliver of steel raced down her spine. She hoped she could live up to his expectations and never hurt his sensitive soul.

Muffled sounds came from inside the house. The light in her mother's room came on.

"I should go see if she needs any help." But she made no effort to remove her hand from where it rested on his arm, covered by his warm, possessive fingers. This new level of intimacy with Michael felt good and right.

"Yes, I suppose I should be leaving." He slowly released her hand. "Would you like me to come by and walk you to church?"

She restrained the desire to hug his arm. "That would be nice." They had sat together for months but always met at the church before the service. "Thank you." Her heart swelled.

They looked into the moon-draped yard, but Chas's thoughts were not on the scene; they were on the man at her side. She wondered if he was thinking about kissing her.

"I'll see you tomorrow." He was gone, like a man fleeing from a ghost.

Chas smiled, understanding how difficult he found it to trust any sort of intimacy, knowing the progress made in their relationship tonight constituted a giant leap for him. It was enough for now. A beginning.

She hurried indoors and down the hall.

Mother was ensconced upon her pillows, the quilt folded neatly across her chest. "Hello, *ma cherie*. Michael has gone home?"

Chas nodded. "He's just left."

Her mother patted a spot beside her on the bed. "Come here."

It was a ritual as old as her life, and Chas sat beside her on the covers. "How are you feeling?"

"I'm fine. I have to learn to be careful, that's all. Forget my old aches and pains. Tell me about your day."

Chas sighed. Where to begin?

"How was your outing with Adam?"

"The falls were lovely. Spectacular. Adam couldn't keep his pencil still."

"He's always so full of the joy of life. It's as if he lives life with a wing and a song."

"Mother," Chas said, chuckling, "you've turned poetic."

"Away with you now. I'm just making an observation." She rubbed her little ivory angel with one fingertip.

"Adam seems—he's such a gentleman. Always so kind to everyone from Mrs. Banner to Emma. Yet—" Again she paused.

"Yet what?"

"Maybe I see it only because I'm your mother." She let the ivory angel lie in her lap, holding it with fingers grown still.

A heartbeat strumming behind her eyes, Chas watched the still fingers, knowing it meant the problem had been sorted. Knowing, too, that her mother was pulling her thoughts into order, praying for wisdom before she spoke.

"Adam appears to have a special regard for you."

Chas said nothing.

"I realize it's none of my business, but has Adam spoken to you of his feelings? Has he expressed more than casual interest?" She rushed on, not giving Chas a chance to answer. "I mention this only because I wonder if I've prepared you adequately for such an event."

Chas laughed. "Are you talking of a man expressing interest? Because if you are, I learned to deal with that by the time I was fourteen years old."

"Chastity!"

"This place is hardly a convent."

"I realize that, but you never told me anyone had ever been—" She stopped, searching for the word.

"Inappropriate?" Chas supplied.

"Were they?"

"Nothing that wasn't handled by a word or two. About all I had to say was, 'Shall I call my mother?' and the miscreant would turn tail and run." No need to mention some of the bigger boys at school who had proved slightly more difficult to dissuade. She was thankful God had always protected her.

"There—you succeeded in making me forget what I was talking about. I suppose that was your intention."

"Not at all. Should I be wanting to?"

"Of course not. I was only wondering about Adam." Again she paused and then rushed on. "But don't feel you have to tell me if you don't wish to."

But Chas wanted very much to tell her mother. "He showed me a sketch of myself. You remember that one he did when I was twelve or thirteen?"

"Vaguely."

"He carried one like it with him all these years." Chas repeated Adam's story, leaving out only the part where Adam said he'd carried her in his heart. Just thinking those words turned her head into a whirlwind of confusion. She knew she would choke if she tried to say them aloud.

"Do you think he's interested in a special way?"

Chas pressed her finger to her chin. "He has no reason to think we're more than acquaintances."

"I wonder if that makes a difference to a man who has thought of you with such high regard for so many years."

Chas let out her breath sharply. "I should think if he truly had feelings toward me, it wouldn't have taken ten years to return and speak of them."

"I expect he thought of you as still being fourteen."

Chas refrained from mentioning one didn't have to be too bright to do the arithmetic. Instead she addressed the thing that mattered most. "It really doesn't matter because I have no desire to be a widow to a man's wanderlust. It isn't at all what I want."

The words fell into silence. Her mother plucked up the tiny angel and again rubbed her finger back and forth over it. After a moment she asked, "What do you want?"

Chas searched for the right words—a way of expressing her desires without making her mother think she was unhappy with the current situation. "I think, most of all, I want to be sure I don't make a decision that would leave me having to make the best of things. I want the very best God has available. And I'm content to leave things in God's hands for His will and His timing."

Her mother clasped Chas's hand. "Chastity, I expect you're talking about my life when you talk of making the best of things. I admit I made a rather big mistake in my youth, and to some it looks as if my life has been relegated to making do, but I don't see it that way. I never have. I feel privileged. After all, I had a firsthand experience with an angel. It turned my life around full circle and gave it meaning above and beyond the ordinary."

Chas was silent. She'd heard it before. She knew her mother believed life had given her a special bequest. But it wasn't enough for Chas. She wanted more. Or, as she had said to Michael, less.

"I never meant to raise you to be afraid of risks."

Chas stared at her mother. "What do you mean?"

"I suppose I'm thinking of Adam. I wouldn't want you to turn him aside simply because of the risks such a relationship carries."

Chas tried to assess her mother's words in light of her feelings about Adam—and Michael. Taking risks was one thing, but throwing everything away recklessly was something else. Besides, it was all a pointless discussion. It was Michael she was fond of—surely love would grow with time. It was Michael who shared a desire for the same sort of life she wanted.

"Are you suggesting Adam might be in love with me? Because if you are, you can put your mind at ease. We are worlds apart. Besides, there's Michael."

"Yes, of course, Michael. Has he given you cause for hope?"

Chas chuckled at her mother's phrasing. Although he hadn't said he loved her or asked her to marry him, he had given her cause for hope. "Yes, Mother, he has."

"Well, he's certainly a solid, steady man. And if that's what you're looking for. . ." Her voice trailed off on a thread of doubt.

"It's what I want—a life that is steady and predictable."

Mother smiled. "Then I can only wish you happiness—whatever you decide." She reached for the Bible. "I rest assured God will direct your steps in the way that is best."

Chas whispered, "That is my prayer too."

Mother read several verses before turning to Chas. "Let's pray together about your future."

Chas let her mother's soft prayer brush clean the hidden corners of her soul like a warm Chinook wind blowing away the accumulated dirt and dust of winter.

Taking with her a fresh settledness, she kissed her mother and hurried to her own room to open her Bible and study the name written on the piece of paper, Simon LaBlanc. What would it have been like to have a father?

&

On Sunday morning Chas set a tray with coffee and toast on the bed beside her mother. "I wish you could come to church."

"I do too, ma cherie, but I couldn't possibly walk that far." She smiled her reassurance. "Now don't you fret about it. Maybe you could mention to Pastor Simpson I'd like to see him when it's convenient." She waved a hand. "Don't look like that. I only want some spiritual refreshment."

"I'll ask him to call."

A few minutes later, she and Michael strolled down the sun-dappled street toward the church. Nothing special happened. Nothing of significance was said. Yet when they stepped through the double doors into the sanctuary, Chas felt as though a sweet bond had been forged. She let Michael lead her to a pew. He sat close enough that their elbows touched. Warmth centered in a place behind Chas's heart.

Emma caught her attention across the room and lifted her hand in greeting. Beside her sat a red-haired, pink-faced youth Chas had never seen before. Then her attention was diverted to the pew in front of them.

"Good morning, Chas." At Adam's warm greeting, she looked up to see the Silverhorn family filing into the pew. Adam was directly in front of her. It was impossible not to notice how his hair—sun-bleached on the ends—curled along his neck. Jack sat at his side, and Adam leaned over to mouth something in his ear, every movement so quick and graceful that, despite herself, Chas found pleasure in watching him.

He turned to face her, and she clenched her hands in a vain attempt to stop the guilty heat from rushing up her cheeks.

"I thought your mother would be here."

She shook her head. "It's too far to walk, and we don't own a buggy or any means of transportation."

"I see." His brow furrowed. "I expect she misses going to church."

"Yes, I'm afraid she does."

Michael said nothing, but the pressure increased along her arm where they were touching.

Pastor Simpson took his place behind the pulpit and called for the first hymn. Chas couldn't help thinking how symbolic it was that she and Michael were joined together by the hymnbook they both clasped. It spoke of so many things they had in common: their faith, their contentment in a quiet life, even their love of teaching children.

Then Pastor Simpson announced the title of his sermon, "The Steps of a Good Man Are Ordered by the Lord," and Chas's attention was riveted on the message.

A short while later, she left the service with her heart lighter, her convictions strengthened. *Thus far the Lord has led me,* she reminded herself. He would surely keep her on the right path.

Emma stopped Chas at the doorway, pulling her aside. "Did you see him?"

"I assume," Chas said, chuckling, "you mean the young man beside you."

Emma grinned. "Remember the old codger cousin of the Simpsons' we were going to meet?"

Chas smiled. "I'm guessing he wasn't so old after all."

"Not a bit old. His name is Gordon Simpson. He's from down east but wants to move west." She grabbed Chas's hand. "Come and meet him."

Chas allowed herself to be dragged to the blushing young man. As she turned to rejoin Michael, she came face to face with Adam.

"Don't forget my opening show tomorrow."

"I'm looking forward to it."

And surprisingly she was. His work, whether photos, paintings, or sketches, had the power to flood her senses with color and emotion. Which did not explain the alarm ringing up and down her spine at Adam's nearness.

"I promised your mother I would bring her more photos to

look at. Tell her I haven't forgotten."

Chas nodded. "I will." And she hurried to Michael's side.

Outside in the warm sunshine Michael asked, "What did Adam have to say?"

Surprised at his sharp tone, Chas said in her calmest voice, "He reminded me he's having his first display tomorrow, and he wanted me to tell Mother he hadn't forgotten his promise to visit her again."

"I suppose that's decent of him."

It was said so grudgingly that Chas giggled. "I suppose it is, though I don't think Mother would want to hear it put quite that way."

Michael had the grace to laugh at himself. "I was rather condescending, wasn't I? I'm sorry. I didn't mean to be."

She tucked his apology and the tiny bit of jealousy he'd shown into her thoughts. Michael was so right for her.

six

Emma spent the morning extolling the virtues of Gordon Simpson, and, according to Emma, he abounded with them.

"He wants to start a new business," she said. "He says he'll spend some time deciding what the town needs." She barely paused as she stepped outside the door to hang the laundry to dry. "He thinks Willow Creek has a tremendous future since it's on the rail line between Calgary and Edmonton." She stepped back inside, the wicker laundry basket under her arm. "Of course the town council has been telling us that for years, and the paper has duly reported it. I just didn't pay them much mind."

Chas hid a smile. As far as she could remember, Emma had only looked at the gossip pages and household hints of the weekly paper. "I'm wondering if you've found Mr. Simpson has a bit more to offer than the local boys?"

It was a longstanding argument of Emma's that there could be no romance with a local boy. "How could I fall in love with someone I've known all my life," she would ask, "and seen with a runny nose or crying for his mama?"

Emma let out a sharp breath. "Do you see any of the local boys setting out to establish a new business? They'll do what their fathers have done and never see what's right in front of their noses."

"So Mr. Simpson is the answer to your prayers?"

Emma blushed. "It's rather soon to tell." She rushed on. "He's not at all like his cousins. He's so—so full of enthusiasm."

Remembering how the pink-faced Gordon could barely say hello, Chas wondered if Emma was the only one who brought forth life in the man.

Emma stopped to study Chas. "Of course I know he doesn't

90

hold a candle to Adam as far as adventure goes, but Adam doesn't even see me. He has eyes only for you."

"Emma! How can you say that?" The room was steaming from the tubs of hot water, and the exertion of running the heavy sheets and towels through the wringer had caused the sweat to bead on Chas's forehead. She paused to wipe her face on a rag.

"I have eyes. And I'm not stupid."

"No, you're not, which is why I'm so surprised you should think such a thing. I could never be interested in a man with wandering feet. Besides, you yourself warned against falling in love with him."

Emma tightened her mouth. "The heart does not always go where the mind goes."

Chas giggled at Emma's stern expression. "True enough, but neither do we have to follow the fickle desires of our heart. I believe in mind over matter—and emotions."

She dumped the rinsed sheets into the basket, and Emma hoisted it to her hip, heading outside to hang them.

"I only hope you don't 'mind' yourself right out of something special."

Chas glanced up. "Special?"

Emma nodded. "I might be young and inexperienced when it comes to love. But I have eyes, and it seems to me one would have to have a weak mind to pass up love—real love— for something 'reasonable.' " She practically spat out the final word and slipped outside.

Chas's startled gaze followed her, and she pressed her lips tight. Why was everyone determined that she and Adam should be romantically interested in each other? She ran a finger under the neckline of her dress to cool herself. Sure, he'd carried a memory of her, but it had nothing to do with reality. She wasn't the person he had carried in his heart all those years. Her dreams and wishes had grown in a different direction from his.

"So what are you going to do about Adam?"

Busy loading the washing machine, Chas spared Emma the barest of glances. "There is nothing to do about Adam. We're old schoolmates, I enjoy his work, and he's been kind to Mother for which I am grateful. We're friends and neighbors. That's all."

Emma sighed, but Chas said no more. Let Emma think what she wanted. Chas knew her heart—and her mind.

But Emma continued. "I suppose you'll end up marrying Michael." She rolled her eyes. "I can see the two of you planning a school program and telling yourself what an exciting day you'd had."

Chas laughed so hard she had to grasp the side of the rinse tub.

Emma glowered at her. "What's so funny? Sounds deadly dull to me."

Chas wiped her eyes on the edge of her apron. "Put that way—it certainly does."

"Believe me, it would be." Emma's forehead wrinkled as she stared into Chas's face. "I sometimes think you're so set on getting a little house of your own that you'd settle on Pastor Simpson himself if he offered it."

Chas giggled at the prospect. "I guess it would work if you marry Gordon and let Martha move in with you."

Emma shook her head. "Not me. Martha goes with her brother."

"I guess that's out then."

"I should hope so." Emma took the last load of laundry and headed to the door. "But I'm not fooling about what I said."

"You really think I should consider Pastor Simpson? He's old enough to be my father."

"No, silly. I mean about having your gaze so firmly fixed on the one thing you think you want that you're blind to everything else." The door slammed shut between them.

Chas shook her head. Young, impressionable Emma would settle for nothing but stars and roses. And gladly live with the consequences. But Chas wanted so much more. It was something Emma, having grown up as she did, would never understand.

❧

The tea had been served and the laundry collected off the line before Chas said to Emma, "I promised Jack I'd go to Adam's opening display today."

"You go ahead," Emma said, glancing up from ironing a sheet. "And while you're looking at the display, have a good look at Adam."

Laughing at her friend's determination, she headed downtown to the shop. Inside she stared around the room. The once bare walls were now colorful with paintings, drawings, and photos. Adam stood speaking to one of the older citizens of Willow Creek. When he saw her, his blue eyes darkened. Then a slow smile drove flashes of silver through his irises.

A sensation stirred in the pit of her stomach not unlike the feeling she had when staring at the whirling waters of Sheep Falls. She blinked to steady herself, blaming Emma for her reaction. She squared her shoulder and took a step forward. Her mind would rule her heart.

"I thought maybe you'd forgotten to come." Adam reached for her hand. "I'm glad you didn't."

An older couple called out, "Adam, where did you paint this picture? It's lovely."

He looked at Chas with regret, then sighed. "Duty calls. Feel free to browse."

She studied the display, entranced by the beauty. Scenery of the Yukon. Weathered faces of its inhabitants. Fleeting glimpses of the wildlife. She circled the room twice and would have gone around again, but Adam was at her side.

"Ellen's going to watch the store for awhile so I can get some air. I thought we might take a walk."

Caught in a web of color and sight and sensation, Chas nodded. If he had asked her at that moment to follow him to the Antarctic, she would have agreed. *So much for mind over matter,* she scolded herself inwardly.

She let him lead her outside into sunshine that was suddenly flat and streets that were colorless and ordinary. A wagon lumbered past, and a child ran across the street squealing in excitement. The spell broken, she planted her feet firmly on the wooden sidewalk. This was Willow Creek, where she belonged, where she longed to make a permanent home.

"Were you pleased with the turnout?" she asked, her feet leading her on a familiar route.

"Yes, very much."

"How did the people respond to your work?" She wondered if others had been as moved by his paintings as she had been.

"Mostly they oohed and aahed. A few asked if they could purchase a piece."

Somehow she couldn't imagine him parting with anything. "Are you selling them?"

"Not from this collection. In a week or two I'll set up a display of work for sale."

They walked past the turreted houses and turned the corner into a narrower street.

"How about you?" he asked. "What did you think of the display?"

She oohed once and then aahed and smiled.

He chuckled. "That good?"

"Yes." She nodded briskly. "I'm not sure I can put it into words, but it was tremendous. I felt as if I were right there. As if I could feel the water's spray, touch the tiny flowers, even smell the sweat on that wizened old man."

"You're doing a good job of putting it into words."

She grinned. "The scenery is beautiful. Somehow I expected barrenness."

Her steps slowed of their own accord as they neared the picket fence. He halted and faced her squarely, blocking her pathway and her view of the little house. "It is beautiful, but in all my travels I found nothing to compare to your beauty."

She raised her startled gaze to his and, at the sight of the glittering warmth in his blue eyes, immediately lowered her head, squeezing her hands into a tight knot.

"I wish I could hang the picture I did of you. Yet I really wouldn't want anyone else to see it. It's the most personal painting I've ever done."

She tried to move around him, but he touched her shoulder and stopped her.

"Don't run away."

She nodded. Perhaps it was best to clear the air.

"I can't imagine life without you." His voice was low and strained.

She took a deep breath. "And I can't imagine living the sort of life you do."

"What do you mean? What do you know about the sort of life I want to live?" His hand was insistent on her shoulder.

She summoned the courage to look him in the eye without blinking. "No doubt, you'll be gone as suddenly as you've come. For how long. Perhaps another ten years?"

He stared at her, his eyes hard and unfathomable. "You're determined to believe that, aren't you?"

"I'm determined not to make a colossal mistake that would ruin my life and rob me of what I want—what I've wanted for a long time."

"I'm guessing you mean me when you use the word 'mistake.'" His words were dangerously low, but she forced herself to maintain eye contact. "And I suppose if I tell you I love you, you'll say I'm incapable of knowing what love is."

"Not at all." She forced the words out of a parched throat. "But it isn't me you're in love with—it's a memory. You don't know who I am or what I want."

His look was cold. "Perhaps you're right. The Chas I remember was never afraid."

She pulled back. "I'm not afraid."

He continued as if he hadn't heard her. "Remember the time you stood up to Carl when he was tormenting little Sally? I can still see you planting your toes squarely in front of him, with your nose practically touching his. I'll never forget how you glared at him and said, 'I don't care if you are bigger than me. I won't let you hurt Sally anymore.' " Adam grinned. "You looked fierce enough to eat him. Poor Carl didn't know what to do. He sort of melted away."

Adam's smile faded, and he grew serious. "Now it seems you wear a pair of blinders so you can't see what's outside your safe little world. When did you become so scared of life?"

Chas had forgotten the incident with Carl, but now the feeling of angry defiance returned. She glared at Adam. "If you'd grown up without a father, always wondering if it was your fault he'd left; if you'd grown up in a houseful of strangers coming and going, asking questions, feeling free to touch your hair and make comments; if you could never have your mother to yourself because of the guests, then maybe you'd understand." She sucked in heated air.

"I am not afraid." She ground the words out. "I only want what I've never had." She stepped around him and pointed at the house. "I want a little home with a white picket fence. A house just for me and my family." With her hands on her hips, she looked at him. "I want a husband who is there for me and our children. I don't want to end up alone—for any reason." She gulped in some air. "I couldn't stand wondering if you would take off again."

Adam touched his finger to her cheek. She hadn't realized she was crying until he wiped a tear from her face.

"Oh, Chas. I can't promise I would never go away, but I would always come back. I love you, and I don't mean that tattered sketch I carried for years. I mean you, all grown up and fierce and gentle and sweet."

She shook away his hand. "You didn't hear a word I said. What we want in life is different." Her voice fell to a whisper. "I can't love you." And ignoring the protest from deep inside her heart, she mentally slammed a door in her mind.

"Can't or won't?"

His words were so low that she wondered if she had imagined them.

"I must go. I have work to do."

She spun around, not caring if he followed or stayed, every pounding footstep she made driving her determination deeper.

At the corner where she would turn one direction and Adam another, she paused.

"Adam, I don't mean to be rude or unkind, but I think it's best this way. I am not the person you think I am. We would never be happy together." She spoke as if he had asked her to marry him, but she had to make him understand. "You're a special person. You deserve someone who shares your dreams and goals, not someone who would always be fighting with them—and you—because of basic differences."

His eyes told her he didn't accept her words, but she still rushed on.

"I hope we can continue to be friends. And I wish you happiness." She held out her hand.

He stared at it as if she had offered a snake and then stuffed his hands in his pockets. "And I hope you come to your senses."

She wiped her palm on her thigh and swallowed hard. "I am being sensible."

He shook his head, a frown carved deeply into his cheek. "By burying your head in the sand? You could end up in a confining, dull existence if you do."

"I don't think that's going to happen."

She rushed toward home until she reached the final corner. She paused to let her racing heart slow down. She knew what she wanted. She would accept nothing else. She marched up the steps and into the boardinghouse.

"How was it?" Emma asked before Chas could close the door behind her.

Feeling as if she'd been caught with her hand in someone's change purse, Chas stared at Emma. "I suppose you could say we sorted things out satisfactorily."

Emma's eyebrows went up. "I meant Adam's show."

Chas adjusted a curtain. "The show was wonderful. He has a lovely collection of pictures of the Klondike. He says he'll leave it up awhile and then put up pictures on gold mining. He says he could pick a different topic every week of the year and change his display to suit the topic."

Emma watched with a wide-eyed expression. When Chas paused to catch her breath, Emma asked, "What was it you sorted out satisfactorily?"

"Things. Nothing. I'm going to check on Mother." She rushed from the room.

"Chicken!" Emma called after her.

The next day Adam appeared in time for tea, carrying a bundle of photos.

"What do you have for us?" Mother leaned forward eagerly.

"Pictures of the Queen Charlotte Islands and the Gulf Islands. I think you'll enjoy the mystic beauty of them."

Chas hung back, not wanting Adam to think she had changed her mind about what she'd said the day before, yet longing to get more than a glimpse of the pictures as they were passed from hand to hand.

"Look, Chastity." Her mother indicated Chas should come to her side. "Isn't this wonderful?"

Chas slid to the chair, hoping Adam would ignore her. The photo was a scene of spectacular mountain beauty and tall trees reflected in glass-calm water.

"I painted the same scene."

Adam handed Chas a small oil painting, and she gasped.

"Adam," Mother said, "I've never had a desire to travel, but these pictures make me want to go sit on this beach."

The beauty was so powerful that Chas felt her heart would explode from her chest. She stood to her feet.

"I have to make a pudding for dessert," she mumbled, fleeing to the kitchen, where she yanked the pot from the cupboard and measured in milk. It was wonderful to see the beauties of the world. She could understand why Adam wanted to travel and see more of them. But she didn't want to think about him leaving again. She was thankful Michael did not feel the same need. He was content to enjoy the pleasures secondhand.

Reason and purpose returned.

Emma joined her a few minutes later. "Why are you in such an all-fired hurry all of a sudden? Did something bite you?"

Chas answered calmly, "Just the need to get supper ready."

"Wouldn't be you're suddenly anxious to avoid Adam?"

Chas shook her head. "I told you there's nothing between us except friendship."

The girl began filling the basin from the bin of potatoes. "By the way, Adam is still in there with your mother."

She shrugged. "It's good of him to spend time with Mother. I know she appreciates it."

Emma sat on a stool and began peeling vegetables. "Why don't you get the rest of the tea things while I do this?"

Chas narrowed her eyes, studying Emma. But the girl was busy with her job, and Chas had no choice but to mumble, "Sure."

Adam and her mother sat with their heads close together, the pictures piled neatly on Adam's knee. As soon she entered the room, they stopped speaking and looked up, their expressions startled.

Chas looked from one to the other. "What are you two up to?"

"I'm going to help Emma," Mother said, struggling to her feet.

Adam jumped up. "I need to get back to the shop."

Chas stared at them.

ã€°

That was the last she saw of Adam for some time, and life settled back into routine.

Michael joined them for supper on Wednesday. They had barely seated themselves around the table when he announced, "Adam has agreed to talk to the students, but he wants to know what subject I'd like him to talk about. What would you suggest?" He addressed the assembled group.

Beryl became dreamy eyed. "The glacier picture, for sure. The mountains and glaciers and rivers of the Yukon."

"That's too vague," Roy insisted. "I'd want to know more about his travels—how long it took him to reach the Klondike and how he did it. A bit about his travels down the coast."

Mother laid her fork down. "Michael, the Klondike gold rush will go down as a significant part of our history. I'm sure Adam could make it a real learning experience for the children."

The conversation went back and forth.

Chas, for her part, silently wished everyone would forget Adam.

Days passed, and Adam did not visit the boardinghouse. Days turned into weeks, and apart from the glimpses Chas had of him seated with his family at church on Sunday, he might as well have disappeared into the wild yonder.

Then one day Emma looked up from washing the dishes. "Adam has a new display at the shop. He calls it 'Faces of the North.' It's very interesting."

Chas nodded. Adam had obviously decided it was best for them to go their separate ways. She agreed. But why was she missing his visits?

"I hear his sales have gone well too. Several parties have come from Calgary and Edmonton for the sole purpose of seeing his display and buying one of his paintings."

"I don't blame them. He's a very good artist."

Emma spun around to face her. "I don't understand you."

"What's to understand?"

"How can you be so dense?" Emma slapped the wet rag over the table. "I had you and him figured out for a sure thing, and now you avoid each other as if you both have something catching."

Chas kept her attention on the platter she was drying. "I tried to tell you we had nothing in common."

Emma exhaled loudly. "He adored you with his eyes. I can't believe you would let that sort of thing go to waste. I know I wouldn't. When Gordon looks at me like that, I'm ready to fall at his feet."

Chas laughed. "Somehow I don't see you turning into a docile slave for anyone."

Emma looked thoughtful. "Knowing someone thinks you're as special as the sun rising makes any task seem like a privilege."

It was Chas's turn to stare. "Why, I do believe you've fallen in love."

Emma's cheeks darkened. She angled her shoulders in an attempt to block Chas's view.

Chas laughed. "I hope he deserves you."

Emma nodded. "I hope I deserve him." Then she straightened. "But you're not making me forget what we were talking about. You must have said something to discourage Adam, for I know he saw nothing, and nobody, but you."

"You're always such a dreamer, Emma. You see romance in every look and conversation. Adam and I are friends, but we are worlds apart when it comes to what we want in life."

"Well," Emma sniffed, "it wouldn't do you any harm to expand your world a little."

"You're impossible. Number one, I have had a very broad experience in life from living in this house. I've met people from all walks of life and from all over the world. Why, right now we have under our roof a man who spent years in the East Indies."

"Oh, I'd forgotten." Emma rolled her eyes. "I suppose you're going to tell me it's been a real learning experience? None of us even knew about our Mr. Elias until Adam showed up." She shook her head, mumbling, "Wonderful things we've heard about the East, I'd say."

"That may be so, but there's something else."

"Yeah, what?"

"As far as expanding my horizons, I wonder how I could do that and still manage this house? You ever think about that?"

Emma was instantly contrite. "I'm sorry, Chas. Sometimes I forget you're stuck here."

"I'm not stuck. This is where I belong."

Emma nodded, her expression thoughtful. "I suppose that leaves Michael."

Emma made it sound like leftover breakfast.

"You are truly impossible." Chas turned away, not wanting her to see how her remark had stung.

Michael had visited regularly as before, but if Chas had expected their relationship to change, she was disappointed. He brought papers for her to help with and news of the children. He reported that Adam had given a talk of the Klondike, and it had been very good. But he had said nothing more about what he had called "being more than friends."

Chas took her restless feelings to bed with her and sat at her little table, pulling her Bible toward her. The page fell open to the piece of paper on which she had penned her father's name. Her heart twisted into a knot, and she rested her fingertip on her mouth. *Simon LaBlanc, who are you? Why did you never care enough to find me?*

❧

Michael came as usual on Wednesday. It took Chas a few minutes to realize he had come without his usual armful of papers.

"Did you forget something?" She glanced down the hall, wondering if he had set them on the table in the entryway.

He shook his head and followed the direction of her look. "I don't think so. What have I forgotten?"

"Where is the children's schoolwork?"

His grin slightly lopsided, he held out empty hands. "No papers tonight." His expression sobered. "I thought we'd just enjoy the evening."

Her heart gave a sudden jolt, and hope swelled in a wave. Then her mother's voice called Chas back to her senses.

"Have a seat, Michael. Supper is served."

Chas barely heard the discussion around the table as they ate.

"Chastity." Her mother's voice was amused. "Have you forgotten dessert?"

Chas leapt to her feet, ignoring the curious stares of those across the table, and hurried to the kitchen. As she dished out rhubarb crisp, she hummed.

After the meal, Michael leaned back in his chair. "I know you like to get the meal things cleaned up right away, so go ahead. I'll have another cup of tea."

Emma followed on Chas's heels. "Don't suppose it occurred to him to help. I'll bet he doesn't even know what dishwater is for."

Chas chuckled. "He must do dishes at home. After all, he lives alone."

"You mean he hasn't invited you to visit him so you can do them?"

"Emma, shame on you. Besides, you know I'd never go to his house."

Emma shrugged. "I guess if you're happy with him waiting for you in the dining room, I shouldn't be concerned. If it was me, I'd want him at least to sit in the same room." She got a faraway look in her eyes, and Chas knew she was thinking of young Gordon, who came frequently to the back door to walk her home.

"I'm happy." It was enough to know Michael was content to wait for her, content to visit at the boardinghouse and not expect her to be free to take time for a bunch of social activities. It was enough he didn't resent her work.

Emma studied Chas's face. "I sincerely hope you are. You deserve every bit of happiness there is."

"Emma, that is so kind." Chas hugged the younger girl.

Emma nodded. "Let's get this finished so you can visit with your Michael." She glanced toward the back door.

"And so you can go out walking with Gordon."

Chas and Michael sat together in the corner of the veranda. The sun dipped toward the horizon, casting ribbons of red, orange, pink, and purple across the sky.

Chas sighed. "There's nothing much better than watching the sun go down on a summer evening." She brushed a strand of hair from her face. Sharing the sunset with someone special made it even more enjoyable.

"You are happy, aren't you?" It was half question, half affirmation.

"Yes, I am. What reason would I have not to be?"

He was silent a moment. "I wondered for awhile if you were greatly disappointed because you couldn't return to teaching."

She continued to watch the sky, the colors dancing into different formations. "I love teaching and would gladly go back, but I'm content to leave things in God's hands and trust His timing. He knows what is best."

"Sometimes He sends unexpected events into our lives."

She nodded, her attention drawn to a sudden flare of orange over the roof of the house across the alley. "Mother always says the unexpected carries a special gift."

Michael laughed a little. "And she's usually referring to you."

Chas turned then to smile at Michael. "She does rather belabor the point."

His brown eyes darkened to the color of rich chocolate. "I don't think that's possible."

Her tongue suddenly uncooperative, Chas let herself float in the depths of his look.

He studied her, his gaze lingering on her hair, her chin, and her lips before returning to her eyes. Somewhat distractedly he said, "I wondered for awhile if you were interested in Adam."

"He's just a friend." Her voice sounded strange in her ears.

"Does that mean I have the right to think you might be interested in me as more than a friend?"

"Didn't we have this discussion not long ago?" It was impossible to concentrate. His look did funny things to her mind.

"Might it be possible for you to consider marrying me?"

The moment froze. She was aware of color dancing across

the sky, bathing Michael's features in a warm golden glow. Her heart throbbed inside her chest. Her emotions curled for a moment and then erupted in a glorious burst of color and joy. She gave one low-throated laugh.

"Michael, if this is a proposal, I want it done right."

His features softened into a knowing smile. "You shall certainly have your wish." He fell to his knees at her feet and took her hands between his. "Chastity LaBlanc, may I have the honor of requesting your hand in marriage?"

She giggled. "Yes. Oh, yes, I'll marry you, Michael Martin." *I'll share your life. I'll enjoy your love. I'll be beside you always and you beside me.*

He stood to his feet and drew her to her feet, their clasped hands against his chest.

She tilted her head back so she could see his dear familiar features. *Michael of my heart.* The words filled her being.

He smiled gently and then lowered his head to touch his lips to hers. It was a kiss as soft and gentle as dew upon the cheek, as pure and undemanding as the summer sun.

And as Chas rested her head against his shoulder, her heart sang with joy.

seven

Chas bounced down on the bed beside her mother.

Mother lowered her Bible and smiled at Chas. "You're looking pleased with yourself, *ma cherie*."

"That's because I'm so happy."

"Something special?"

Chas turned to her side. "Something very special indeed. Tonight Michael asked me to marry him."

Her mother nodded. "And I take it that you've accepted."

"Of course."

"Then I'm very happy for you. Michael is a nice young man, steady and dependable." She leaned over and kissed Chas's cheek.

The familiar scent of her mother's dusting powder filled Chas's nostrils. "I'm very lucky."

Her mother lay back against her pillows and sighed. "I guess we'll have to begin making plans. Have you picked a date?"

Chas laughed. "I never even thought of it."

"Yes, I suppose you had other things on your mind."

She gave her mother a startled look, but the older woman's face was innocently expressionless. "It was so unexpected." Chas stared up at the ceiling. "He was so sweet."

Her mother chuckled low in her throat. "One would rather expect him to be at this point."

Chas giggled. "One would, I suppose."

Mother grew thoughtful. "I hope you can put off your marriage until I'm well enough to take over the boardinghouse again."

Reality slammed into Chas's chest, driving her breath from her. For a moment she had flown away on her dreams—

marriage, a little house of her own, raising a family with Michael. But now the cold hard facts had to be faced. Her mother wasn't able to run the house on her own and may never be. If only she would sell the place—perhaps now she would consider it.

"I know what you're going to say. You want me to sell." Her mother picked up her little ivory angel from the bedside table. "To you it makes sense, but I can't. Not yet. It's too final a choice. I can't even contemplate it."

"I know how much it means to you," Chas said. "And to be perfectly honest, Michael and I never even discussed a wedding date. But I promise I will not leave you to manage on your own. Somehow things will work out. God will provide a way. Isn't that what you've taught me all my life?"

Mother grasped Chas's hand. "I have indeed, *ma cherie*. And I know He will. Let's turn it over to Him."

Chas closed her eyes and bowed her heart before God as her mother prayed aloud, first thanking God for sending Michael into Chas's life and then laying out the problem before Him. "God, from the moment You sent an angel to rescue me, You have never failed to provide my every need, and I know You won't fail me now. I'm asking You to meet our need, and I'm suggesting the best way would be for my leg to get better. Thank You. Amen."

Chas giggled.

Her mother raised an eyebrow.

Grinning, Chas explained. "I was thinking how funny it is for you to tell God how He should answer your prayer. Maybe He has a different plan in mind."

"If He does I'm sure it's better than mine, so I won't have any trouble accepting it."

Chas laughed at her mother's pleased-as-a-cat expression.

They remained there quietly. Chas let contentment slide through her. The future was as bright as the stars in the sky. Suddenly she jumped to her feet, pausing to kiss her mother's cheek before she went to her own room, where she did a little dance across the narrow space, hugging herself as she drew to a halt in front of the table.

"Thank You, God," she murmured, picking up her Bible. Dropping to the chair, she read a few verses and let the pages fall open to the piece of paper bearing her father's name. She stared at it for a second and then picked up the bit of paper and pressed it to her chest.

a

The next morning Chas greeted Emma before the girl got through the door. "Guess what?"

Emma closed the door behind her and faced Chas, looking her up and down slowly. "Someone left you a fortune?"

Chas pulled herself taller. "Nope. Something better."

"Your mother sold the boardinghouse?"

"Not a chance." Chas stepped aside to allow Emma to unhook an apron from behind the door and tie it around her waist.

"Then Adam must have come calling."

Chas jabbed her fists to her hips. "You couldn't be further from the truth. Michael asked me to marry him."

Emma dropped to a chair and stared at her. "So he finally got around to it?"

"You make it sound as if I've been waiting for ages." She thought Emma would have been a little more enthusiastic.

But then Emma sprang to her feet and threw her arms around Chas. "I'm very glad for you. When's the big day? Where are you going to live? What's to happen to the boardinghouse? And your mother?" She pushed away and studied Chas with wide eyes. "Wow! I can't believe it."

Chas laughed. "He only asked last night. We haven't had a chance to discuss any of the details." She sobered. "I guess the most important thing is Mother's needs." She took a pot holder and removed six golden loaves from the oven. "Somehow things will work out."

"I'm sure they will." Emma picked up a pot and filled it with water. "I guess this means Adam is out of the question?"

"Oh, you." She flicked a towel at Emma. "He's a free man as far as I can tell. If you're so interested—"

Emma gave her head a toss. "I've already found what I want."

The girls grinned at each other.

"Life is good, isn't it?" Chas said, as she tipped the loaves onto a clean towel.

Around the table that evening, Emma, having asked Chas if she meant to keep her engagement a secret and being told no, said to the assembled group, "Chas has some very special news."

Every eye turned toward her. Chas wished Michael were there to share the moment, but he wasn't, and she had no choice but to answer the babble of questions.

"Michael and I are going to be married."

Beryl bounced forward. "Congratulations, Chas. I'm sure you'll be very happy."

"Yes, congratulations," Louise said.

John added more slowly, "He'll be staying on as teacher then?"

"Thank you." Chas smiled at the two girls, then turned to John. "I would assume so."

Mr. Elias sat up straighter. "May I add my congratulations? Young Michael is a good man. I'm sure you'll be very happy."

Mrs. B tugged at Mother's arm. "What's all the fuss?"

Mother leaned close. "Chastity announced her engage-ment to Michael Martin, the young teacher who visits here."

"Michael Martin, you say? Isn't he that quiet young fellow who comes and goes all the time?"

"The teacher, yes."

Mrs. B sat back and squinted at Chas. "Well, I declare."

Chas smiled at the old lady, having no idea what her comment meant.

Roy leaned forward and asked in a cautious way, "What about the boardinghouse?"

The quietness following his question told Chas the answer

was important to everyone at the table. "We have made no plans as yet, but selling the house is not something we're considering."

She felt the room swell with a collective sigh of relief.

"I'm planning to continue running this place even after Chastity marries." Her mother's look told them she would contemplate no other option.

"But, Miz LaBlanc, what about your leg?" Beryl asked, her voice filled with concern.

"We would make other arrangements if it came to that," Louise added, her voice soft.

Mother waved away their concern. "I'm expecting to get better faster than any of you think."

Even the Knutsen boys looked up with sudden interest.

"We all hope you do," Beryl said and asked for the bread to be passed.

As if by some signal, the conversation turned to other matters, and Chas knew no one wanted to argue with her mother about her chances of getting better.

❧

Chas knelt in the warm dirt of the garden, plucking weeds from around the pea plants. The sun was warm on her back. The birds sang from the tree branches, their songs ringing through her heart.

After a while, Chas sat back on her heels, turning her head about to ease her muscles. The beautiful Saturday afternoon would soon be more glorious when Michael arrived. She hadn't seen him since he'd proposed. Each evening she had hoped he would come, and when he failed to appear, she had consoled herself with the knowledge he was busy with year-end tests and preparations. Suddenly she chuckled. It had been all of two nights since she'd seen him, and here she was acting as if it had been weeks.

She bent back to her task, a smile on her lips.

"Chas?" A familiar voice called her name.

Her heart leapt to her throat, and she turned around. Adam

stood at the gate, his arms resting on the top bar, his hands hanging over into the yard. She stared at his hands—long fingers, flecks of red and blue paint under his nails.

She stood to her feet, dusting her skirt.

They were several feet apart, but not so far that Chas failed to see how dark his eyes were.

"Hello, Adam." She brushed her hair out of her face. Why was he here?

He watched her without speaking.

She took a step and another, bringing her within reach of the gate. She halted, twisting her hands together. Now she could see smudges of green on his thumb and a black mark on his index finger.

His hands pulled away, and she looked up. His eyes glittered with silver. "I had to come and hear for myself."

"Hear what?"

"That you and Michael are getting married."

The tension drained from her, and the sun was again warm. She smiled. "Yes, we are."

He nodded. "Then I wish you every happiness. I hope he loves you very much."

"Thank you." She paused. "How are things at your shop?"

He rubbed the top of the gate post. "Good. Very good."

She couldn't think of anything more to say.

He cleared his throat. "I've come to tell you I'm going away for awhile. I'm taking my display on tour across Canada."

"I'm not surprised. I always knew you'd be leaving sooner or later." The news didn't upset her. She had Michael's love to protect her.

"I hadn't planned on leaving so soon, but suddenly it seems like a good time."

She knew he meant because she had agreed to marry Michael.

"I'll only be gone a few weeks. I have shows lined up down east, Winnipeg, Toronto, and a few other places." His eyes found hers.

She knew he still hoped she'd give him a reason to stay. But she couldn't. "I hope you have a good trip."

"Maybe you'll be married by the time I get back."

"Maybe. We haven't discussed a date yet." She shrugged. "There are a lot of things to consider."

"Of course." He glanced past her to the house. "Say goodbye to your mother for me, will you?"

"You're welcome to tell her yourself."

For a moment he looked at the house and then shook his head. "No, you tell her."

"I will."

His gaze found hers again, and she gasped at the stark emotion in them. Then he blinked, and his expression deadened. "I'll miss you."

She nodded. He meant more than the impending trip, more than her engagement to Michael. He was saying good-bye to a dream he had carried for the better part of ten years. She saw the pain in his eyes and wished she could do something. But there was nothing left except to say good-bye.

"Have a safe trip," she murmured.

He gave a tight smile. "And you have a good life."

He looked at her a moment longer, as if memorizing every feature, and then turned and walked away.

She stared after him a long time. Finally she muttered, "There was never anything to miss," and returned to weeding the garden.

Later, as she prepared for supper, she made frequent trips to the dining room window to check for Michael's arrival.

"Why don't you set the table while I mash the potatoes?" Emma finally said. "That way you won't have to make so many trips into the dining room." She shook her head. "I've never seen you so anxious for visitors."

Chas wrinkled her nose. "It isn't just any visitor. It's Michael." At Emma's raised eyebrows, she added, "I know he's been coming every Saturday for months, but now it's different. Now I can't wait to see him and see if he's still the same or"—

her voice was muffled as she pulled aside the curtain—"if he's changed." Her voice dropped so low she knew Emma couldn't hear. "As I've changed." Suddenly Michael was so dear, so important she half expected him to have grown several inches.

Finally she saw him coming. If he glanced at the house he would see her waiting, but he turned in at the front gate and headed for the door without looking in her direction.

Chas raced for the door, throwing it open before he could give the bell a twist. "Michael. I thought you'd never get here." She leaned forward, lifting her face for a kiss.

"Am I late?"

"No, I was only anxious to see you." She waited, her face upturned.

"Well, I'm awfully glad to see you too." He dropped a kiss to her lips, warm but so short she swallowed her disappointment.

"Come on in. Supper's ready." She pulled her hand through the crook of his arm as they walked to the table.

Besides her mother, only Mr. Elias, Mrs. B, and the Knutsen boys were there.

Mr. Elias stood and offered Michael his hand. "Congratulations on your engagement, my boy. You'll make a fine couple."

Carl and Orsby each mumbled their congratulations without lifting their heads for more than a moment.

Chas drew Michael to her mother's side. Mother took one of Michael's hands, looking at him with a keenness that made him stiffen.

"You're a fine young man," she said. "I'll expect you to take good care of my daughter. Always."

Michael held her gaze a moment. "Yes, Ma'am. I aim to."

He smiled at Chas, and she knew she had never seen anything as wonderful as the way his expression softened as he looked at her.

"Good. Now everyone sit, and we'll have our supper."

Chas was grateful the others weren't with them. It allowed her and Michael to eat in peace without the questions she knew they would direct at him—questions she and Michael hadn't yet had a chance to discuss.

As soon as the dishes were put away and Emma had departed with a waiting Gordon, Chas drew Michael out to the veranda. They sat elbow to elbow on the bench, Chas letting the peace of the evening envelop her, hoarding to herself the joy of Michael at her side.

It was Michael who broke the silence. "Your mother sounded as if she doesn't like me much."

At the injured tone of his voice, Chas placed her hand on his forearm. "Oh, no, Michael. She likes you fine. She's just protective of me." Chas sighed. "I guess it comes from her being my only parent. She feels she has to do everything twice as well. But don't take it personally."

He nodded. "It's not as if I don't intend to take care of you."

"I know that. So does she. I told her about us last night, and she was pleased about it, so stop worrying."

He took her hand, sliding his fingers between hers. "I will then. After all I don't want to ruin such a nice evening and the company of such a beautiful girl." He beamed at her.

His eyes were as warm and gentle as liquid chocolate, and she let herself float on her dreams. "Don't be looking at me like that, Chas."

He tweaked her on the nose, and she giggled, shifting on the bench to look out on the yard.

"Now that you've had time to think about getting married, are you having any second thoughts?" he asked.

"Of course not, Silly. You and I will make a fine match." Only one thing would make her happier than she was this moment—for him to say how much he loved her.

"We will, won't we?"

She rested her head on his shoulder, sighing. "We have so many things to discuss."

He pulled back. "We do? Like what?"

"Now it's you who's being silly. We have to decide when we're to be married, where we'll live, what to do with the boardinghouse. All that sort of thing."

He remained quiet so long that Chas shook his arm and asked, "Have I overwhelmed you?"

"No. It's just—" He cleared his throat. "I sort of thought it was pretty obvious."

Her mind went round and round seeking answers. How could he have found them so quickly and simply? She shook her head. "It's certainly not obvious to me."

Smiling, he continued, "Probably because you're too close to see what's right in front of you."

"So explain to me what I'm not seeing."

"Let's take things in order. First, when should we marry? I propose we marry as soon as I've finished teaching for the summer.

"As to where we'll live—why, this house is ideal." He pressed her hand to stop her from arguing. "You and I can move into the private quarters. Your mother could move into the room she insists on keeping empty. It's time it was put to good use."

"It's for emergencies."

Her mother insisted the small room next to Mrs. B's be kept unrented so they could offer it to people in distress.

"We must be prepared to take in strangers," she insisted every time the subject came up. "We never know when we might be entertaining angels. Or simply helping travellers in distress—'as ye have done it unto one of the least of these.' "

The room had been used numerous times over the years.

Once a young woman went into labor on the train, and Chas's mother had taken her in and cared for her and the new infant until the frantic husband could be contacted to come and get his wife and new son.

Another time, an elderly man rode into town, hungry and befuddled, and her mother had nursed him until he was strong again and could remember who he was. They never knew for sure what happened. Her mother said he must have banged his head somehow.

Then there was the young couple, their wagon on its last legs, their money gone. Her mother had allowed them to stay until he earned enough money for repairs so they could continue their journey.

Others had stayed there as well.

Michael waited for her response.

"I don't know what Mother would say."

"I'm sure she'll see the reasonableness of it."

"You think we should continue to operate the boardinghouse then?"

"Of course. It makes good money, and it isn't too much work." He turned toward her. "You don't mind the work, do you?"

She shook her head slowly. It wasn't the work she minded. With Emma's help she managed very well. No, it wasn't the work at all.

"Good. Then it's all settled. I told you it was simple."

He made it sound so reasonable—all the problems taken care of. Except one. "But, Michael, I thought we'd get a place of our own."

He turned and stared at her. "How would you manage the boardinghouse?"

She plucked at her skirt. "I hoped Mother could be persuaded to sell it," she mumbled.

He sat back. "I never even considered that. You've discussed this with your mother, and she agrees?"

Chas's heart sank through the seat of the bench. "She flatly refuses to sell."

"I'm confused. I don't understand why you think your mother should sell this place. It's a prospering business. Besides, how often have I heard you say you're perfectly happy here? Why would you want to change that, especially when it's plain that your mother has no intention of selling?"

She shrugged, at a loss for words. As plainly as Michael had just expressed them, her wishes appeared silly and juvenile. She swallowed hard.

"I guess it's only a childhood dream."

Ignoring his puzzled look, wanting nothing more than for him to understand her desire, she forged ahead. Even if they were left with no choice but to live here, she ached for him to acknowledge the yearning of her heart.

"All my life I've dreamed of living in a little house all my own, sharing it with no one but my husband and children." Her voice fell to a whisper. "All I want is a place of my own."

His brown eyes were puzzled. "I guess we wouldn't have to run the boardinghouse all our lives." He smiled gently. "Someday you'll get your little house."

She nodded, knowing she would have to be content with his promise of "someday."

"Don't look so disappointed." He pulled her close, tucking her head under his chin. "Things will work out. You'll see."

With a contented sigh, she relaxed against his chest. After a moment, she pushed away and lifted her face. "Michael, you have a way of putting things in perspective. You're so good for me."

He lowered his head and gave her a warm, gentle kiss that settled through her.

A few minutes later he said good-bye, and Chas crossed the kitchen toward the rooms she shared with her mother and would in a few weeks share with Michael. Her steps faltered. What would Mother say about his proposed arrangement?

She paused in the doorway, half hoping her mother had fallen asleep already, but she glanced up. "You have something you want to discuss, *ma cherie?*"

Chas lifted her hands in a gesture of resignation. "It's impossible to hide anything from you."

Her mother smiled. "Of course, I'm your mother." She patted the bed at her side, and Chas hurried over, sitting down so she could see her mother's face.

"Michael and I were talking."

"You've made some decisions?"

Mother's face was smooth, giving away nothing. Chas took

a deep breath and began.

"Michael wants us to get married as soon as he has finished teaching for the summer."

Her mother nodded. "I see."

"He wants to move in here. He means for us to live here." Chas's throat tightened as she said the words.

Her mother looked at her, waiting for the rest.

Chas dreaded saying it. "He thinks we should make this our room. He says it makes sense for you to move to the guest room beside Mrs. B." Her words came out in a rush, and then she sat there, breathless, watching her mother's reaction.

Mother looked around the room. Her eyes widened. Then she sighed. "It will take some getting used to." Then she turned back to Chas. "How about you?"

Chas lifted her eyebrows.

"It's been all 'Michael says this' and 'Michael wants that.' Are you happy with the plans?" She patted Chas's arms. "Before you answer, remember I'm your mother and I see things others don't."

Chas swallowed hard, determined she would not make this any harder for her mother than it already was. "I don't suppose it will come as any surprise to you that I someday hope to have a little house of my own."

"I know, *ma cherie.* I've always known."

Chas waited for her emotions to calm before she continued. "I don't know why it seems so important."

Her mother stroked her hair. "Perhaps it's because so many things have been missing in your life."

Chas drew back. "I certainly don't think that. You've always been here for me."

Mother nodded. "Thank you. But you've missed a family. A father." She sighed. "And you've had to share everything with the boarders. Even your mother. And though you've always been sweet and nice about it, I can't help thinking it's created an emptiness inside you that may never be filled."

Chas lay back. Could it be true that this longing, this

emptiness, would never be satisfied? "It doesn't make sense. I'm not unhappy. I feel as if I'm trusting God. I try to. Why should I long for things that will never be mine?"

Her mother tucked Chas's hair behind her ear. "Perhaps you are reaping the result of my bad choices."

Chas looked at her. "What do you mean?"

Mother shrugged. "I was so desperate for someone to love me and take care of me that I married Simon without knowing who he really was. If I'd taken more time to figure out what it was I wanted and to get to know him, things might have turned out differently. And you're the one who has had to pay for my mistake."

"Mother!" She grabbed her mother's hand and squeezed it. "I've never suffered. In fact I always thought I was luckier than most people to have a mother who cared so much and who taught me to trust God wholeheartedly. Things will work out somehow. I know they will."

Her mother gave a low laugh. "Now it's you who's reminding me to trust God." She picked up her Bible. "He will never fail us."

Mother read a few verses, and then they prayed together.

Chas silently mouthed the words, *God, help me be content in the place You have put me.*

ও

The days fled past. Michael kept busy in the classroom and Chas in the garden.

One morning, well into June, Chas returned to the house from weeding and pulled off her gloves when the front doorbell rang.

"I'll get it," she called to Emma, who was ironing sheets.

"Yes?" she asked, as she opened the door to a tall, thin man, neither old nor young. "May I help you?"

"Miss LaBlanc?"

"Yes." It wasn't unusual for people to have been given the name of the owners of the boardinghouse.

"I need to speak to your mother." He coughed—a cough that

shook his frame and made him grasp the door post. He sucked in a rattling breath. "I have something for her—for you both."

Chas noted bright red spots in each sunken cheek.

The man swayed. Chas grabbed him, clutching at his sleeves. "You're sick!"

She turned and called over her shoulder to Emma, hoping the girl would hear the urgency in her voice. Something clattered in the kitchen, and Emma was at Chas's side.

"Help me get him into the spare room."

Emma grabbed one elbow. Together they steered the tottering man down the hall and shuffled him through the door to the edge of the bed, where he collapsed on the covers.

"What is it?" Mother called from the kitchen.

"Just a minute, Mother," Chas said, then to Emma, "I don't want her coming in here until we know if this man has something contagious." She lifted the man's legs to the bed and pulled off his scuffed boots.

"Right."

They stood at the bedside looking down on the man.

He regarded them from fever-glazed eyes. "I don't want to put you to any trouble."

Chas smiled. "It would appear you're the one with the trouble."

He nodded, tried to say something, and had a coughing spell. Finally he gasped, "Thank you for your kindness."

Emma turned to Chas. "Do you want me to get Doc Johnson?"

"Yes, please. And if he isn't in, leave a message."

Emma hurried from the room.

Chas studied the gaunt man. Without his hat, she could see he had thinning blond hair. From the way his clothes hung, she guessed he had been sick a long time.

"What's your name?"

He tried to smile. "Colin Courtney. Please call me Colin."

"Do you have any family I should contact?"

He shook his head, too weak to speak.

Chas patted his shoulder. "You rest. I'll go tell Mother what's going on and then bring you some water. And not to worry. You can rest here until you're better."

"You're very kind," he whispered as she slipped away.

Mother was standing up from her chair when Chas hurried into the kitchen. "Mother, what are you doing?"

"I was going to see what all the commotion is about."

Chas explained about the visitor and that he was now resting in the spare room. "I want you to stay away until we know what's the matter. There's no point in everyone's coming in contact with him if it's something contagious."

Her mother gave her a hard look and pursed her mouth, preparing to argue, then relented. "I suppose you're right. Have you sent for Doc?"

"Emma's on her way."

"Good." Mother sat back. "No matter what is wrong with the poor man, he's going to need lots of fluids. And some broth. Do you still have the chicken bones from Saturday?"

Chas smiled to herself. She might succeed in keeping her mother from the sickroom, but she couldn't keep her from playing nurse from a distance.

"I'll take him water right now. By the way, his name is Colin Courtney." Chas paused, remembering. "He said he had something for us. I wonder what it could be?"

Mother looked up, interested. "I don't know the name." She turned away. "I can't imagine what it is."

As Chas supported Colin's shoulder so he could gulp the cold water, Doc Johnson trundled into the room. "You run along for a few minutes, Chastity, while I have a look at our patient." He dropped a dusty satchel on the floor and lay an equally dusty coat on top. "I found these on the step. I presume they belong to your guest."

"Thank you," the man muttered. "I guess I dropped them."

"Now you lay back and behave yourself while I check you over." Doc waved Chas aside and sat on the edge of the bed, his bulk making the springs protest shrilly.

Chas hurried back to the kitchen. Emma already had the chicken simmering on the stove. She glanced up at Chas's entrance. "Doc was full of questions, but I said I didn't even know the man's name."

"Colin Courtney."

Chas put the kettle on for tea and took out a tray, her hands busy even though her thoughts were centered elsewhere. When Doc called her name from the bedroom, she set the creamer down and hurried to the bedside.

"Beside being too thin, the man has a dose of pneumonia. He'll need some good nursing to pull through." Doc shook his numerous chins. "That's where you've found your bit of good luck, my man. You couldn't find a better place to get good nursing. Chastity and her mother have provided care to strangers many times over the years."

The weakened man nodded.

Doc turned to Chas. "I took it for granted you'd be taking care of him here."

"Of course. Where else would the poor man go?"

Doc rolled his lips like a bull frog. "I've taken the liberty of removing his shirt and pants."

The man lay under a thin blanket.

Doc Johnson picked up his black bag. "I'll leave this syrup to calm his cough. Give him lots of fluids. Sponge him to bring the fever down. Call me if he worsens. Otherwise I'll drop by tomorrow. Good luck, my man."

When Chas started to follow him to the door, Doc said, "No need to show me out. You've got your hands full here."

Emma could manage tea and the rest of supper preparations, leaving Chas free to care for the sick man. As Doc had said, Colin would need good nursing to fight his illness.

She hurried to the kitchen for a basin of water and cloths to sponge him down.

eight

Colin coughed until it seemed his thin frame would break. Finally the cough syrup took effect, and he fell back on the pillows, the perspiration pouring from him.

Chas sponged his forehead, his neck, and his shoulders. "Your sheets are soaked again. I'll have to change them before you can rest." She hated to make him move for fear it would start another bout of coughing.

"I can't thank you enough." His voice was tight, and she knew it took an effort to say even those few words.

He rolled toward the wall, and Chas pulled out the sweat-soaked sheet, tossing it toward the door. Then she pulled the clean one tight and tucked it in place. He lay back, and she spread a light blanket over him and smoothed it across his shoulders.

She arched her back to ease her sore muscles and noticed the sky had turned slate gray.

Colin followed the direction of her gaze. "Almost morning," he whispered. "I've kept you up all night."

At the regret in his voice, Chas shook her head to clear away the fog of sleepiness. "It wasn't your fault." He had alternately shivered, sweated, and coughed. "Besides, I managed to get a little sleep." She nodded toward the armchair.

His smile was weak. "Not very much, I'm afraid." He took a heaving breath. "I think I'll be able to rest now, so you go and get some sleep."

Chas assessed his color. Despite the bright spots in his cheeks, his skin had a gray cast to it. He clutched the covers to his chin, and she knew it was the beginning of a chill that would lead to a rise in his fever. "I'll rest in the chair for a bit."

His eyes thanked her.

"Don't worry." She squeezed his hand. "I'll see you through this. You won't be alone. I promise you."

His eyelids closed, and he took a deep breath.

She tiptoed to the chair and stretched out, pausing only to ask God to heal Colin's frail body before she let sleep claim her.

She woke to the sun shining through the window and pulled herself up in the chair. Colin's covers were tossed aside. His skin glistened with sweat. He tried to stifle a cough, but when she stood, he let the cough rack through him.

His sheets were soaked again. As soon as he stopped coughing, she changed his bed and added the wet sheets to the growing mound outside the door.

A few minutes later, Emma came with hot tea. "How's the patient?" she whispered.

"About the same." Chas nodded toward the pile of sheets. "I'm afraid you'll have to do laundry today. I expect he will need nursing most of the day. Do you suppose you could get someone to help you?"

After a moment of consideration, Emma nodded. "I'll see if Dorothy can come. What about you? Did you get any sleep?"

"A bit." She pushed her hair off her face, realizing how rumpled she must look.

"I'll relieve you after I get things organized."

Chas nodded, shutting the door behind Emma. Colin seemed quiet for the moment, and she again settled into the chair.

The day passed with Colin alternately shivering and sweating and always racked with coughing. Chas changed his sheets and continually offered fluids.

Early in the afternoon, Emma came to the room.

"Dorothy and I have everything under control. Run along and get some sleep."

Chas headed to her room, pausing only long enough to tell her mother about Colin's condition.

The second night was a repetition of the first.

The next day saw no change in Colin.

Doc Johnson came by to check on him. "You're doing all you can," he told Chas, shaking his head in a less than assuring way.

Chas prayed even harder for Colin.

His gaze followed her every time she stepped away from his bedside. Sensing he did not want to be left alone, she pulled her chair close and asked, "Would you like me to read to you, or would you prefer I sit quietly?"

"Talk to me." The few words triggered a coughing spell.

As soon as he quieted, Chas told him about the meal Emma was preparing, about Dorothy helping. She described the yard and the weather. He clung to every word. When his eyelids drooped, she thought he had fallen asleep; but when she stopped talking, he opened his eyes, silently begging for more.

So she told him about the boarders and her mother.

Again Emma came to the door in early afternoon to allow Chas a few hours of sleep.

She returned to the sickroom refreshed, and Emma hurried out to complete supper preparations.

"Talk to me some more," Colin begged.

So Chas told him about growing up in Willow Creek, about life in a small town, about going to school. Somehow she ended up telling him about Adam and his drawing.

A short time later, Emma returned to the door. "Michael's here asking for you."

Chas blinked. "Is it Wednesday already?"

Emma nodded.

"Where is he?"

"Cooling his heels in the sitting room." Emma paused. "I better warn you—he wasn't pleased to hear you'd been nursing a stranger night and day."

"Really?"

Emma gave her a thoughtful look before she ducked into the kitchen.

"I'll be back in a few minutes," she told Colin, closing the door softly.

In the sitting room, Michael stood with his back to her, his arms crossed as he looked out the window. She watched him for a moment, seeing nothing in his stance to indicate displeasure.

"Hello, Michael. I'm sorry I was busy."

Michael spun around, his face wreathed in a wide smile. "You're here now. That's all that matters." He strode to her side, taking both her arms and pulling her close. His expression darkened as he looked down at her. "So what Emma says is right. You've been nursing that man night and day. I can see it in the dark shadows under your eyes."

She shrugged. "He's very ill."

"How did he end up here?"

"I have no idea." She recalled how he'd said he had something for them and wondered what it was. "Maybe someone sent him."

"I suppose they knew he'd be welcomed here even if he was sick with who-knows-what."

His tone made it clear he thought it was an imposition. He held up his hand. "Don't deny it. Everyone knows your mother has a reputation for taking in strays."

She faced him squarely. "It's a noble reputation."

"I suppose it is." He sighed. "Though not one I should think we need to continue."

She stared at him. Where did he get the "we"? Last time she checked, this was still her mother's house. Did he think he would become owner and operator when they married? She closed her eyes and took a deep breath. It was fatigue, she reasoned, making her overreact to his innocent statements.

"Never mind now." Michael led her to the couch and pulled her down beside him. "I've missed you."

Her annoyance fled. "And I've missed you." She settled back against the cushions and sighed.

"I don't like this." He frowned. "You're all tired out."

"I'm fine."

But at that point Colin coughed. Chas leapt to her feet. "I

better get back to the sickroom."

Michael grabbed her hand. "Let Emma do it."

Chas shook her head. "She's got her hands full. Besides, it's not her responsibility."

Michael was insistent. "Nor is it yours."

"Mother has taught me well." Chas faced him. "I could not turn my back on a stranger in distress."

He stood to his feet. "Chas, enough of this foolishness!"

She stared at him, stunned by his reaction, longing for him to understand and support her. But all she saw was the tightness of his mouth.

"I'm sorry," she mumbled. "But it's something I have to do."

She tore from his grasp, racing down the hall. Michael would have to accept her decision. She pushed her disappointment to a dark shelf of her mind.

For three more days Chas nursed Colin through raging fever, shuddering chills, horrific sweats, and hacking coughs, each day wondering how much longer his body could endure.

Her presence seemed to calm him, and he asked her over and over to talk to him. "I like the sound of your voice," he choked out between coughs, "and hearing about you as a little girl."

So she dredged her memory for stories of her childhood—the time she locked herself in Mrs. Allan's henhouse and had to wait, sneezing and scratching until Mrs. Allan came to free her. She laughed, remembering the louse bites she suffered.

She told of the time she had stood up for little Sally, the time Adam drew her picture, and so many things she hadn't thought of for years.

Michael came again Saturday, waiting in the sitting room for her to slip out.

"Michael," she began, "I'm sorry, but I can't leave Emma there for long. She has supper to serve."

He gave her his stern teacher look. "This has gone on long enough."

"I agree," she said, purposely misinterpreting his comment. "The poor man has endured enough."

"You can't wear yourself out taking care of him. It sounds to me as if he may not even make it."

"He's not going to die," she vowed, pulling in a deep breath. "And if he does, he'll not do it alone and uncared for."

Michael threw up his hands. "He's only a stranger."

" 'I was a stranger, and you took Me in,' " she quoted, not willing to admit that Colin was more than a stranger. Over the past few days a bond had grown between them. In many ways he was the father figure she had never known. She would not abandon him to the ravages of his illness. Not even for Michael.

"I'm sorry. But try to understand—this is something I must do." She paused. "You're more than welcome to stay for supper, but I won't be available."

She waited, hoping he would relent, but his face remained stern as he silently challenged her. She turned and left the room.

That night Colin worsened. Chas did her best to fight the fever, but it continued to rise alarmingly.

Having exhausted her resources, she could do nothing but fall at his bedside and pray. *God, You are the great healer. Please touch Colin's body and heal his illness.* She prayed for a long time until she rose and resumed her nursing, believing God would answer.

Toward morning the fever began to fall. Just as dawn threw pink banners across the sky, he took a deep, shuddering breath. She pressed her palm to his chest, relieved to feel it rise.

The worst was over.

Thank You, God, she breathed.

She sank into the chair and slipped into an exhausted sleep, not waking until Emma came in dressed in her Sunday best. Chas scrambled to her feet.

"I forgot about church."

Emma laughed and pushed her back down. "Too late now. It's all over."

Chas leaned her head against the back of the chair. "I can't believe I slept right through."

"You needed it. How's our Colin?"

Chas's smile felt as wide as the open sky as she studied him still sleeping peacefully. "His fever broke early this morning."

"Praise the Lord," Emma said. "I expect it will take awhile to get his strength back."

Chas didn't answer. It was enough for now that Colin was on the mend. She followed Emma from the room, joining her mother and the others for lunch. She was surprised to find Michael wasn't there.

"Where's Michael?" she asked Emma. "Wasn't he at church?"

Emma gave her an odd look. "He was, but he said there was no point in coming over when you were otherwise occupied."

"Oh." She couldn't help being disappointed. "Perhaps he'll come this afternoon."

"Could be." Emma opened her mouth as if to say more but stopped herself and set out the cold chicken.

Chas helped carry out platters of food. "By the way, what are you doing here today?"

Emma lifted one shoulder. "I figured you needed the help."

"Emma, you are such a dear."

The younger girl chuckled. "I know."

❧

Michael called that afternoon, coming when Chas was in the sickroom spooning chicken broth into Colin.

She slipped away to speak to him, aching to smooth over their misunderstanding. "Thank you for being patient," she began as soon as she stepped into the room. "Colin is over the worst now."

"Does that mean you're finished looking after him?"

"Not exactly." She smiled gently. "He's very weak."

Michael turned away.

"Michael." Chas reached for his arm. "Please try to understand."

"That's just it. I don't understand. I'm sure Doc could find someone else to look after him."

"Michael, it's part of who I am. It's a culmination of my history and how I was raised."

He looked down at her a long time, his brown eyes dark and troubled. Finally he smiled. "I guess if that's who you are, then that's how it must be."

She longed for him to heal her trembling emotions with a hug and a kiss, but when he made no move to do so, she lowered her eyes, forcing herself to be content with the victory she had won.

Except to drink sweet tea and swallow a bit of chicken soup, Colin slept for two days. He woke the third morning to give Chas a slow smile. "So my nurse is still here."

"As long as you need me." She studied the steadiness of his pale blue eyes, the slight pink in his cheeks. Now that the fever had left, she could see that he was probably in his forties, a serious-looking man with a kind face.

"You've been a faithful nurse. I think I might owe you my life." His smile deepened. "Thank you."

"You're most welcome. Now how about some nourishment? What would you like?"

"Now that you mention it, I am hungry. Breakfast would be good."

"I think you'll have to start easy," she said a few minutes later as she returned with thin oatmeal and toast.

"This looks fine." He looked up from the tray. "Won't you sit down and visit while I eat?"

She welcomed his invitation. Over the passing days she had found satisfaction in sharing the story of her life with him.

He waited until she sat down before he bowed his head and prayed out loud, thanking God for his healing, for Chas's faithful nursing, and for the blessing of food to replenish his strength. He took several mouthfuls of the oatmeal before he turned to her. "You've told me so much about yourself that I feel as if I know you. So forgive me if I seem presumptuous in the way I talk."

She smiled. "I feel the same—though I know very little about you."

"There's not much to know about me." He tilted his head. "I'm just a wandering old man."

"I expect there's more to it than that. How did you end up here?"

A strange light filled his eyes. "Divine intervention, I expect." He studied her seriously. "I notice Doc calls you Chastity though everyone else calls you Chas."

"Mother never calls me anything but Chastity."

"It's an unusual name."

"Very." She laughed. "You see, when my mother was expecting me, she ran away from a bad situation. Lost and alone, she was rescued by a man she declares was an angel. She vowed to live a life devoted to serving God and anyone He sent across her path. She named me Chastity to remind her of her vow."

"And your father?"

"I never knew my father. I didn't even know his name until a short time ago. Simon LaBlanc."

"What happened to him?"

"My parents married down east and then moved west." She twisted her hands together. "After they moved, Mother said my father changed. He started drinking and grew violent. She ran away from him and never heard from him again."

Chas had learned to live with it and accept it, but at the compassion in Colin's kind, steady gaze, she clenched her fingers.

"So you grew up wondering if your father was alive and if he knew about you. Wondering too, I'd guess, why he didn't care enough to find you?"

Emotions she had hidden from all her life sprang loose, choking her, sucking at the depths of her soul. Hot tears poured down her cheeks. She dashed them away.

"Didn't I matter?" she gasped, unashamed for Colin to see her this way.

"Of course you mattered. You always did and always will. You are a special young woman. Kind and gentle, sweet yet strong. Not to mention beautiful. Everything a young woman should be."

She clung to his words, letting them ease through her pain like a healing balm. "I've never allowed myself to admit how much it hurt that my father didn't care about me."

"Perhaps it has affected you more than you think."

She blinked. "Why do you say that?"

"You grew up strong. Yet I think a tiny bit of you is locked away, afraid of the future."

She thought how similar his words were to what Adam had said. "I don't see how wanting security indicates fear."

"It doesn't, as long as wanting security doesn't disable us from embracing the future."

Again she shook her head. "Why would I want to choose anything but security?"

"You wouldn't want to necessarily, but remember—security means being free to take a risk."

Although uncertain what he meant, Chas nodded.

"Now I seem to recall a young man wanting to see you several times. Tell me about him."

"Yes, Michael. He's the teacher." She told him everything she could think of about Michael. "We're going to be married soon."

"Then he must be a very special young man. I hope he loves you very much."

"He is."

She faltered. Michael had never said the words, "I love you."

"I'm sure he loves me."

"Love is patient and kind. It always protects, always trusts, always hopes, always perseveres."

He spoke the words like a benediction, and Chas nodded, certain Michael loved her that way. Even as she loved him.

Colin pushed aside the breakfast tray. "I had a bag when I came. Do you know where it is?"

"In the closet. Would you like it?"

"Yes, please."

She set the tray on the floor outside the door and retrieved the bag.

"Would you get your mother, please? I have something for her."

Chas tilted her head. "Of course."

"Colin wants to see you, Mother," she said as she set the tray on the table.

Mother pushed herself to her feet and, using two canes, headed toward the bedroom. "Probably wants to discuss rent. As if I'd charge someone for being sick."

Her mother was gone a long time, and when she came out, she did not return to the kitchen, heading instead for her bedroom. She only paused to say, "Chastity, Colin would like to see you."

A sheen of tears coated her mother's cheeks, and her voice trembled.

"Are you all right, Mother?"

The older woman nodded. "Go see him, Chastity."

She hesitated. Then curiosity drove her toward Colin's room. She pushed open the door. The skin on his face was taut as if the meeting with her mother had sucked out all his energy. He lifted a shaking hand.

"Come in, Child." He waited until she perched on the edge of the chair. "I have looked for you a long time to bring you a message from your father."

A jolt raced through her veins. Could her father be asking for her after all these years?

"First, let me tell you what I know of him.

"When I met Simon LaBlanc," Colin began, his voice soft and low as if he meant to tell her a long story, "he was a broken man, sick and injured. But most of all his mind was not at ease. During the weeks I tended him, he told me his story.

"I will tell you it as I remember it."

Colin paused. "I ran into him way up north. He'd taken to

trapping. Lived alone in a little cabin up along the Mackenzie basin. This particular time he had headed to the Hudson Bay post to trade his furs and get a few supplies for the winter. On the way he ran into some varmints of the two-legged variety who had tried to take his furs off his hands without offering to pay for them. He managed to dissuade them but was shot up. By the time he reached the post, he was more dead than alive with a bullet lodged inside his chest and one leg already gangrenous."

Chas stared as Colin told a tale of fighting and injury such as she had only heard of in tales of the Wild West. To think her own father had been involved in such was beyond her imagination.

"It took several of us to persuade him to let us take care of his furs and quite a few attempts before he would let them out of his sight so we could carry him to my cabin. I did the best I could for his injuries, but we couldn't do much for his leg or the internal wounds. I think he knew. That's why he insisted I hear his story. This is how I remember it.

" 'I've lived a life of regrets,' he told me. He was a big man, with a wild black mane of hair, who had fought every kind of danger known to man, but his eyes filled with tears as he spoke. 'I married a fine young woman, and I done her wrong. When she left me, I didn't even try to find her. I got me a child somewhere, and I don't know if it be a boy or a girl. Don't know if it's got black hair like me. Or maybe white blond like my own mother, God rest her soul.' "

Colin grew quiet a moment. "Before Simon died, he wrote a letter to his wife and child and made me promise to do my best to deliver them. For awhile I wondered if I'd be able to keep my promise, but here I am." He reached into his bag and pulled out a worn and soiled envelope. "This is his letter to you."

Hands trembling, Chas took the letter. A tightness around her lungs made each breath difficult. One fingertip caressed the envelope. She closed her eyes as if doing so could contain the whirl of emotions racing back and forth through her like a washing tide. Having suddenly and unexpectedly found her father through Colin's story, she just as suddenly had lost him again. This small bit of paper was all she had left. She sought Colin's gaze, clinging to the steadiness of his light blue eyes.

He smiled and nodded. "Your father lived all those years wishing he had done things differently, wishing he could go back and undo his mistakes. In the end"—Colin's low voice deepened—"in the end he found his peace the way we all have to—he turned to God and sought forgiveness there."

The stillness around them was alive with images of Simon LaBlanc.

"I don't know what he said in his letter to you, but I do know he would have asked for your forgiveness."

Chas's vision blurred. Choking back a sob, she hurried from the room, seeking the shelter of her own narrow quarters. She flung herself across her bed and sobbed, but she couldn't tell if she cried over the pain of her father's death or the gladness that she had this bit of him to touch and hold.

She wiped away her tears and turned the envelope over. She ran a fingernail under the flap. The paper crackled as she drew forth the pages and unfolded them. Strong black letters marched across the yellowed paper. Chas drew in a shaky breath and began reading.

To my child,

I don't even know if you're male or female. All I know is I've thought of you so often over the years. You may wonder how I can say that when I never went lookin' for you or your mother. But it's true.

You might ask where I was and what I was doin' all this time. It's not a pretty story, but mostly I was drinkin' and soberin' up. When I got tired of that, I headed north. I found a little peace in the aloneness up here—a peace that was haunted by rememberin' a woman and child I had let go.

If you get this you'll have met Colin. He told me I

*could make peace with God. I have, but my mind won't
rest until I tell you I'm sorry. If I could go back, I'd do
things a lot different.*

*I'm not thinkin' you can forgive me. Maybe it wouldn't
even be right, and I don't deserve it.*

*I do wish for you to be happy. Maybe you never think
about me, but if you do, don't have any regrets. And don't
ever live your life lookin' back, wishin' things might have
been different. Don't make the mistakes I made. I thought
I could live without love. I was wrong. If you find someone to love, that is the most important thing you can find.
Never let it get away from you.*

God bless you.

> *From your father,*
> *Simon LaBlanc*

Chas pressed the page to her lips. "Simon LaBlanc," she
whispered. "My father." A shuddering breath escaped. "I forgive you. I guess I always have." And someplace deep inside
her, an empty and hollow place filled with warmth.

Someone knocked on her door. "May I come in?" her
mother asked.

"Yes," Chas answered, suddenly anxious to know how her
mother had received this news.

Mother shuffled in, leaning on her canes. "You have read
your letter?"

Chas sniffled as she nodded. "How are you, Mother?"

"I'm fine," she said, smiling. "I'm so glad Simon found
God in the end. He says he never quit loving me, and that
makes me feel good. It's you I'm concerned about, *Cherie*. To
hear from your father so suddenly after all these years—it
must be a shock."

Chas gave a tremulous smile. "It's a nice surprise. I'm so
glad he wrote me a letter." She hugged the pages to her.

"Does it answer a need inside you?"

Chas, laughing low in her throat, hurried over and gave her

mother a hug. "I suppose it does. But don't go thinking that means I've been unhappy, because you know I haven't."

"You have always been a happy, contented person." Her mother pressed a kiss to her cheek. "Always so sweet. I couldn't ask for more."

"I love you, Mama."

"And I love you, Chastity, *ma cherie.*"

Chas smiled at her. "Now do you suppose I should go see about supper?"

"I think Emma has it under control, but perhaps you should see if Colin can be persuaded to eat a bit."

Colin was watching the door as she entered. "I've been waiting for you."

She smiled. "I'm fine if that's what you're worried about."

"You've been crying."

She nodded. "But it was a good sort of crying."

"I never could understand that sort of thing." He chuckled, his pale eyes warm as the bright summer sun.

"Thank you for going to all the work of finding us and bringing us news of my father."

"It was not as difficult as you might imagine."

They heard a knock on the door, and Emma stuck her head in. "Michael's here asking for you."

"Ah. The young man. He's been patient long enough. You run along and visit him." Colin settled back and closed his eyes. "I believe I'll rest."

"Thank you, Colin," she whispered.

Michael sat in a hard chair, his feet planted on the floor. He smoothed his tie and straightened his lapels as she entered. "I take it the patient is on the mend?"

"Yes, he's much better. Thank God." She burst to share the news Colin had brought, yet the new feelings were too fresh. They needed a chance to mature and stabilize. And so she hesitated.

"Good. I didn't like having to share you with him." Michael crossed to her side and pulled her into his arms, his words muffled against her hair. "I want you all to myself."

His words trickled down her spine, vaguely troubling. How could he expect to have her all to himself if she were to run the boardinghouse? She smiled against his shoulder.

"I'd like that too."

She hoped he would realize how impossible it was under the present circumstances and suggest they consider alternatives, but he only hugged her.

"So Colin will be leaving?"

"He's too weak to get out of bed."

"Are you telling me your nursing duties aren't over?" he asked, pushing her away so he could look into her face.

She stiffened. "They aren't as demanding as they were."

He dropped his hold on her and stepped away. "I hoped I wouldn't have to say this, but it seems I have no choice." His blunt fingers rubbed across his hair. "I cannot accept the way you devote yourself to him." Eyes cold, he faced her. "I will not play second fiddle to a stranger. I insist you find someone else to care for him."

She shrank back as if he'd threatened her. "That's ridiculous."

How could he be so high-handed? Caring for others was part of running a boardinghouse. Certainly, the time she had given to Colin's care was above the norm, but in some circumstances, more time than usual was demanded.

"What if it were Mrs. B who was sick?" Suspicion flared. "What if it were Mother?"

He refused to answer.

She refused to look away. "Is it Colin you object to or having to put yourself aside for an evening or two?"

"He's been here ten days."

Chas blinked. Since when did Michael keep track of her daily activities?

"Because if it's just Colin, you're being ridiculous. He's brought Mother and me a message."

Michael's contemptuous snort made her glad she hadn't told him anything more.

"How very convenient." He glowered at her and then took a deep breath and started to plead. "Chas, try to understand. I've hardly seen you in over a week."

She breathed hard. She should be flattered by his words, but suddenly they sounded petty, possessive. "If you'd needed me for anything, I would have done things differently, but—" She threw up her hands. "Colin, on the other hand, was very ill. I could hardly let Mother take over his care."

"He's better now. You said so yourself. So are you going to do as I ask and find someone else to give him the extra care you insist he needs?"

"It sounds very much like an ultimatum." She spoke quietly.

He half shrugged. "I suppose you could look at it that way."

She took a step toward him. "Michael," she pleaded, "it doesn't have to be this way."

He drew back. "Are you refusing to do as I ask?"

She stood helpless and confused. Perhaps she could find someone to care for Colin, but she didn't want to; she wanted to spend as much time with him as possible, asking about her father. Besides, she'd grown close to Colin during his illness. She didn't want to turn his care over to someone else. For some unfathomable reason, she needed to do it herself.

Michael waited, stern and unrelenting. Michael, her dearest friend. How could he demand this of her?

She shook her head. "Michael, please understand. I must do it."

He stepped away. "Then you leave me no choice but to withdraw my offer of marriage."

Her knees gave way under her. She reached out to the tea table for support.

"Michael, no."

"I fear you are not the person I thought you to be. When I marry, I will not share my wife with another man. Not for any reason." He walked out of the room without a backward glance.

Chas sank into the nearest chair, moaning.

nine

Fearing someone would come into the room and wonder why she was huddling in the chair, Chas squared her shoulders and headed for the kitchen to prepare a tray of chicken noodle soup and custard for Colin.

He gave her a surprised look when she entered his room. "The young man has left already?"

To her chagrin, she burst into tears.

Colin said nothing as he waited for her to stop crying.

"He said—it was—over," she managed to say between sobs. "He—doesn't understand."

"I see." Colin pulled himself up on his pillows. "What is it he doesn't understand?"

"Me," she said, fresh tears welling up in her eyes.

"Well, that is rather important in a relationship such as yours."

Chas, hearing the smile in his voice, took a deep breath. "I'm sorry," she muttered. "I didn't mean to do that."

Colin's smile was gentle, his voice soft. "I don't imagine it's the sort of thing one plans to do. Now tell me what happened."

She shrugged, suddenly discovering she had no idea how to answer him. "He withdrew his offer of marriage."

"Sounds like a lover's quarrel. If he really loves you, he'll be back soon, apologizing for being so silly." He gave her a hard look. "One would assume he does love you?"

She couldn't meet his gaze. "I'm sure he does. He just never thought to tell me."

"What!" Colin exclaimed. "I should think it would be uppermost in his mind. I would expect him to be so overwhelmed by love he couldn't stop talking of it."

Chas could feel his gaze upon her like hot flames, but she

140

refused to meet his eyes, afraid he would see more than she intended.

"What about you?"

His soft tone did not deceive her. She knew he was probing her depths. She squirmed.

"What do you mean?" She made her eyes tell nothing as she faced him.

"Do you love him?" Before she could answer, he added, "Or does he feel safe to you?"

A wave of confusion swept through her.

"Ahh." Colin nodded. "So that's it."

"No. I don't know. Maybe. We are good friends. Michael and I have a lot in common. We think the same. Or at least I thought we did."

"Were you perhaps seeking the security you never knew from your father?" He didn't wait for an answer. He didn't seem to want one. "Don't be misled. Security is not necessarily found in taking the safe, comfortable path. God has created you with a heart full of dreams. Follow your heart. Don't quench your emotions."

Her thoughts swirled. Questions she had never dared to ask raced through her mind. Had she accepted Michael's proposal simply because it felt safe? Because Adam's confessed love frightened her with its inherent risks—and its intensity.

"I'm so confused."

Colin squeezed her hand. "Change is often frightening."

She clung to his hand. Life had turned on its side.

"Chastity, God will guide you, but you must be willing to step out in faith. Now you run along and let me rest."

She sprang to her feet. "I've taken too much of your time."

He laughed, a soft, pleasing sound. "I seem to have a great deal of time right now. I'll pray for you to be able to sort out what it is you want."

She murmured her thanks and hurried from the room.

&

Chas sat on her mother's bed.

"Something's troubling you, *ma cherie*. Is it hearing from your father?"

Chas swallowed back a sob. "Michael says he's changed his mind about marrying me."

"But why?"

Michael's resentment and his ultimatum poured forth.

"Did you explain that it's always been our policy to care for strangers in distress?"

"I tried. He knows the angel story. He should understand. The really unfair thing is he insisted it was wisest for me to keep running the boardinghouse after we married. He wouldn't even discuss other options."

Tears pooled in her eyes, but she was too drained to cry.

Her mother pulled her into her arms, and Chas cradled her face against her neck, breathing in the scent of rosewater and powder.

"Chastity, I'm so sorry." She waited a moment. "But I have been praying you would make the right decision. I wouldn't want you to make the kind of mistake I made. Far better you sort these things out ahead of time. If he loves you, he'll be back."

"That's what Colin said too."

In her own room, she sat at the little table, opening her Bible to the page where the name, Simon LaBlanc, stared up at her. She unfolded his letter and lay it beside the Bible. And over it all, she mentally placed the name Michael Martin.

How did it all fit together?

If you find someone to love, that is the most important thing you can find.

The sentence from her father's letter jumped out at her.

Love. Love protects, perseveres, trusts, hopes. Was it love she felt for Michael? Or safety?

Was she looking for something she had missed as a child? Was she afraid to take risks because of that lack?

Why did Adam keep popping up in her mind?

Because you refused his love out of fear.

The words blared through her thoughts.

She stared into her heart.

Adam had confessed a deep, passionate love for her, and she had run away because it frightened her. She didn't want to live with his need to visit strange new places.

He had never promised he wouldn't go away. He had only said he would come back.

And that had scared her.

But would Adam be Adam if he didn't have a hunger to see and know and record everything he saw? Could she ask him to be anything less?

Love trusts. Love perseveres.

She ran her fingers along the page of her father's letter, letting his words of counsel sift through her consciousness.

It was too late to think about how things might have been with Adam. But it was not too late to be honest about who she truly was and what she wanted.

She was her father's daughter as much as her mother's. She wanted love. She wanted trust. And while she was being truthful, she could not deny she wanted a little home of her own with a husband and children. Michael was comfortable, but it seemed he was not able to give her the things she wanted any more than was Adam.

Father God, You know my desires. You know me better than I know myself. Guide me in the right direction.

෴

The days passed. Colin slowly gained strength and began getting up.

Michael did not return.

Chas admitted what she felt for him had not been love, yet she missed his visits terribly. She missed hearing about the children and discussing lesson plans. After several Sundays of seeing him at church and aching at the way his glance slid away from her, she sought him out after the service, catching up to him as he headed home.

"Michael, can we talk?"

He paused, his back to her. She thought he was going to walk away without answering. Then he turned around slowly. "Certainly."

She fell in step beside him, suddenly not knowing what to say to him. "How have you been?"

"Fine."

"I suppose you're preparing the final report cards for the class?"

"Yes."

She sighed. "This isn't going the way I'd hoped."

He stopped and faced her. "What had you hoped?"

She searched his face for some sign of what he was thinking, but his eyes were guarded, his expression controlled. "I was hoping you'd agree to be friends."

He stared at her.

"I've missed our visits." She rushed on. "I think we were both mistaken in thinking we could be anything more than friends. We want different things, but still we share a lot of common interests." She faltered. "I guess I hoped we could go back to before."

He laughed. "Before our ghastly mistake, you mean?"

She nodded uncertainly.

His eyes darkened. "You aren't mad at me for being so pigheaded?"

It was her turn to laugh. "Of course not. You only made clear what was happening. We're good at being friends but not much good at planning marriage." She waited as he relaxed.

"Friends?" She held out her hand.

"Yes, friends." He clasped her hand for a moment. "Now tell me how you are and how things are at the boardinghouse."

As they meandered home, they filled each other in on the events of the past few weeks. At the last corner, Chas drew to a halt. "Michael, be honest with me."

He nodded. "I'll try."

"You never really loved me, did you?"

He looked sheepish. "I was hoping to find someone who

loved me more than anything else in the world—in a way I've never known." His voice grew husky.

"Michael." She hugged his arm. "I'm sorry I couldn't be that person, but someday she'll come along. And you'd better be waiting for her."

"I hope you're right."

"I'm sure I am."

She stared down the street. What Michael wanted was what she wanted. Probably what everyone wanted. Would she ever know that sort of love? A pair of glittering blue eyes sprang to her mind. Adam said he loved her. But was it only part of some fanciful dream he had carried for years? She closed her eyes and took a deep breath. What did it matter? She had turned him away, and he had left, perhaps for another ten years.

"Come for dinner," she said to Michael. It would help keep her mind occupied.

&

A few days later Colin announced, "Thanks to the good care and excellent food I've enjoyed, I am fully recovered. It's time I was on my way. I'll be leaving on Friday."

His words echoed around the table. All eyes turned toward him.

Beryl bobbed forward. "Mr. Courtney, why must you leave? I'm sure there's something here you could find to do."

"I have things I must attend to."

The Knutsen boys dipped their heads in unison and resumed eating.

"Are you sure you're quite well?" Louise asked.

"I'm fit as a fiddle."

"A man must do what he has to do," Mr. Elias said. "We will certainly miss you."

"Where are you planning to go?" Roy asked.

Chas could see Roy's mind busy with how far, how many days, how long.

"I'm heading west." Colin's smile was gentle. "There's someone I must find." He looked into Chas's eyes. "I will certainly miss this place."

She lowered her head, afraid she would cry in front of everyone. It was impossible to imagine life without Colin; he had come to mean so much to her.

"Don't feel you have to rush away," Mother said.

Chas waited until supper was cleaned up and Emma headed home before she sought out Colin. He was sitting on the veranda steps, his back against the post, gazing into the sky.

She pulled her skirt around her legs and sat beside him. She didn't speak. There was no need. All she wanted was to be with him and cherish his presence.

After a few moments she murmured, "I wish you didn't have to go."

"I do too."

"Then why go?"

He touched her shoulder. "Because I must."

She drew in a breath.

"Chas, I will never forget you. I will pray for you every day. I wish you all God's best and every happiness."

"Thank you," she said faintly.

He squeezed her shoulder. "If I had a daughter, I would want her to be exactly like you."

A sob caught in her throat.

He smiled. "My dear, remember—follow your heart. It will guide you to love and happiness."

She nodded.

They sat under the stars for a long time. Then Colin rose.

"I think it's time to get some sleep." He helped Chas to her feet. "Don't be afraid of the future, my child. God will guide you."

"Good night, Colin." The door closed softly behind him before she whispered, "Good-bye."

On Friday, Chas and Emma prepared a special meal for Colin's farewell dinner. Michael and young Gordon Simpson had been invited.

"Isn't this exciting?" Emma put the finishing touches on

the trifle she'd prepared.

Chas tried to smile. "You mean Gordon coming?"

Emma held her hands over the whipped cream a moment before she turned to face Chas. "I was forgetting about how you're feeling. You'll miss him, won't you?"

"It won't be the same with him gone." Chas lifted her shoulders. "It's like losing one of the family."

Emma's eyes softened. "I'm sorry."

"It looks as if everything is ready." Chas stirred the gravy. "Have our guests arrived?"

At that moment the back doorbell sounded, and Emma stepped over to admit Gordon. Then the front doorbell rang, and Chas hurried to open the door for Michael. Everyone was there. There was no delaying the inevitable, and she announced supper.

Somehow she got through the evening, and the next morning she managed to wave good-bye to Colin without breaking into tears. She watched him ride out of sight and for a long time stared down the road after him. Then she returned indoors, thankful she had a meal to prepare, the garden to take care of, and shopping to do.

Two weeks later, Louise announced, "I saw Adam at the shop today."

She gave Chas a long look, but Chas only nodded and smiled as her heart did a funny flip-flop. She hadn't expected Adam to return so soon.

Beryl edged forward. "I expect he's got lots of interesting tales to tell. I wonder if he'll come visit." She slid a look at Chas.

"I do hope so," Mother said. "He's such an interesting young man."

Mrs. B looked up. "Why do you want a fan? It's not hot."

Mother smiled as she leaned close and yelled in Mrs. B's ear. "We were talking about Adam."

Mrs. B's eyes widened. "I remember him. His folks run the store. Such a nice young man." Smiling, she picked up her fork and turned back to her food.

Mr. Elias perked up in his chair as if he'd been waiting for Adam's return. "I have some things I would like to discuss with him."

"How long was he gone?" Roy squinted his eyes, mentally figuring it out. "Six weeks. Say, he could have gone"—more mental measurements—"why, he could have gone to the East Coast and back in that time."

The Knutsen boys turned in unison from one speaker to the next as if they were of one mind.

John added, "I heard he's planning a big show here. Seems some VIPs are coming to town to see him."

Roy almost jumped from his chair. "How many are coming? When?"

"Who cares?" Beryl interrupted. "Goodness. One would think numbers are everything."

Roy frowned, shifting back. "I was only wondering."

"Perhaps Adam will come for tea, and we can all have our questions answered." Mother turned to Chas. "In fact, why don't you slip down to the shop and invite him? Tell him how much we'd like to see him."

At her suggestion, Mr. Elias beamed, but the young people looked disappointed because they wouldn't be present at that time of day. Seeing their reaction, Mother chuckled. "I'll be sure and invite him for dinner the first evening he has available."

The Knutsen boys bowed their heads over their plates. Chas did the same, not wishing to face any questioning glances, not wanting to face her own swirling emotions.

≈

She would have ignored her mother's directive to issue an invitation to Adam, but shortly after lunch the next day, Mother reminded her, "Be sure to drop by Adam's shop while you're getting the mail and ask him to come for tea."

She met her mother's look squarely, wondering if she were more eager to visit with Adam or to play the matchmaker?

Mother smiled, her eyes guileless. "I'm sure he's full of interesting stories of his travels."

"No doubt."

Chas shook her head. Her mother didn't fool her. But Adam was not the man for her; he was a wanderer at heart. Nor was Michael, who sought someone he wouldn't have to share. Was she doomed to live forever in a boardinghouse, caring for and serving strangers rather than having a family of her own?

Stepping into the sunshine lifted her spirits at once. God would guide her steps as surely as He had put the sun in the sky. It was hard to be patient, but she knew God's timing was best.

The door of Adam's shop was propped open to let in the summer breeze. Chas stepped soundlessly over the threshold and stopped.

His back to her, Adam was leaning over his worktable absorbed in some papers. He hadn't heard her enter, allowing her a chance to study him unobserved. His hair had lightened in the summer sun. A recent trim left a narrow white edge around his hairline. The way he leaned on the table made his shoulders seem broad while revealing his leanness.

Chas swallowed back an aching emptiness. He was good and kind. In many ways he was all her heart desired. Except for one fundamental thing. He had not nor, she suspected, ever would promise he wouldn't do any more traveling. And she could not give her heart to a man only to wonder every day when he was leaving. She couldn't love him. She wouldn't.

Follow your heart.

She had promised Colin she would, but it was a promise she couldn't keep. Squaring her shoulders, she vowed she would protect her heart. As she stepped forward, she spoke.

"Hello, Adam."

He lifted his head, staring at the wall in front of him a moment, and then turned slowly. "Hello, Chas."

His smile didn't quite reach his eyes. His eyes darkened as his gaze swept over her, taking in a wayward strand of hair, resting for a moment on her chin, then descending to her dusty shoes.

Her tongue stiffened, and no words came.

His gaze returned to her face, his eyes slightly narrowed. "What can I do for you today?"

She lowered her gaze to her twisting fingers. She noticed that her fingertips had turned white, so she relaxed her hold. Taking a deep breath, she forced her thoughts to the invitation she had come to deliver.

"My mother asks you to come to tea at your convenience."

He nodded his head in acknowledgment. "How is your mother?"

The tension seemed to leave her, and a slight smile formed on her lips. "Mother's fine. She's getting around with both canes and, as often as she can elude my supervision, using only one." Taking another breath, she smiled more warmly and went on. "I sometimes wonder if I were noncompliant when I was a child and now I'm reaping what I sowed."

Adam's smile brightened, and his eyes warmed. "Were you?"

"Not that I recall. I think I was more likely to retreat to my room than defy my mother."

"Not very confrontational, are you?" He leaned one hand on the table.

"Only when I feel it's worthwhile."

"Like defending someone else, I suppose?"

Not knowing how to answer, she chose to ignore his remark. "I didn't expect you back so soon."

He crossed his arms over his chest. "It was six weeks."

Her glance slid over the pictures on the wall behind him.

"Did you expect me to disappear into the beyond and never return?"

She shrugged. "I guess I didn't know."

"I told you I was going on tour. I didn't plan to be gone long."

Chas could think of nothing to say in response.

"How are your wedding plans coming? The big day must be close now."

She looked sharply at him. "I thought you would have heard." Everyone in town knew.

His face gave away nothing. "Heard what?"

"Michael and I have decided we're more suited to being friends than husband and wife."

His expression never changed.

"It was quite amicable," she murmured.

"Friends?"

She nodded.

"You don't love him?" He was so impassive she wondered if he even breathed.

"Only as a friend."

"I see."

What did he see? she wondered, feeling compelled to explain. "We discovered we really had different goals and expectations."

"Are you saying you didn't love each other enough to reconcile those differences?"

Her eyelids twitched. He made it sound mean-spirited and selfish whereas it had been, as she said, amicable. "I guess you could put it that way if you want to." Her terse tone indicated he would be wrong to do so.

"It's none of my business, I know, but I'm curious to know exactly what you found to be such a big difference you couldn't work out."

For a moment she was tempted to tell him it was indeed none of his business, but something in his eyes made her answer. "I think Michael discovered I was not the malleable person he hoped to have for a mate." She shrugged. "And I did not wish to be confined to his set of parameters."

"It sounds to me as if you're saying neither of you was willing to accept the other as you are."

She nodded. "I suppose that sums it up."

He strode to the window. "Then I guess it was never true love." The light sharpened his features and painted streaks through his hair. "It seems to me that true love accepts the other person just as that one is and wraps love softly around the beloved without binding or constricting."

Chas couldn't breath. A tiny pulse hammered against her left temple. Soft love. It sounded like a dream too good to be true. Love trusts.

At that moment Jack bounded into the shop. "I've done my chores, Adam. Dad says I can help you." He skidded to a halt. "Hi, Miss LaBlanc. How are you? What do you want me to do, Adam?"

"Hi, Sprout. Give me a minute, will you?" Adam shoved his hand through his hair, looking as if he wanted to say more to Chas.

But she had turned and dashed out the door.

 za

Chas set out the tea things, wishing she could avoid meeting Adam somehow. His words haunted her; they condemned her. She understood that as Michael had wanted to confine her to his own expectations, she had done the same to Adam. Her fear wanted to bind him to certain rules. Yet she didn't know how she could do otherwise; her heart dreaded making a mistake she would regret the rest of her life.

She knew she must sort out the problem in order to love the way she wanted to love and be loved. If not with Adam, then with the man she would trust God to provide.

When the bell at the back door rang, she grabbed the teapot and hurried to the dining room, calling to Emma to let in their guest.

Emma mumbled something about running away and then called for Adam to enter.

Chas kept busy handing out tea, making sure Mrs. B's was quite correct and her mother had the little table close to her knee. She hoped if she took long enough, Emma would wait on Adam. But today Emma seemed inclined to passing out the cookies slowly, forcing Chas to hand Adam his cup.

"Thank you," he said quietly.

Unable to stop herself, she glanced up. His blue eyes

glittered knowingly. She dropped her head, ignoring his low chuckle.

"I won't bite," he murmured for her ears alone.

His comment was so unexpected that she pulled back and laughed. "Then I promise I won't either."

It was that easy to make a truce, and Chas relaxed and settled back to listen to his tales.

"I feel it was a very successful tour," he concluded. "Mr. Edwards of Calgary, a prominent businessman, has organized a group of other businessmen and notables to come here to Willow Creek and see more of my work." He managed to look uncomfortable and pleased at the same time.

"That's wonderful, Adam," Mother said. "I expect they'll want to buy as many pictures as you care to part with."

Adam laughed. "Thank you, Miz LaBlanc."

Mr. Elias excused himself, heading for the stairs. He surprised them all a few minutes later when he reentered the sitting room and marched to Adam's side. "I have something I want to show you." He unwrapped a parcel and pulled out a book, handing it to Adam.

Adam read the title out loud: *"Memoirs of a Soldier,* by T. L. Elias. Why, Mr. Elias, you've had your life story published."

Mother sat forward. "How thrilling! You wrote it yourself, Mr. Elias?"

He nodded.

"So that's what you've been working at?" Chas asked, giving an I-told-you-so glance to Emma.

"It's taken me a long time," Mr. Elias said.

Adam was still examining the book, reading excerpts aloud, when Chas followed Emma to the kitchen.

"A book. Can you imagine?" Emma was obviously vexed no mystery was involved.

"It sounds as if he had a very interesting life."

Emma sighed. "I had so hoped it was something a little more dramatic."

Chas laughed. "Seems to me life is complex enough without

looking for something to complicate it."

Emma considered Chas. "Are you referring to anything in particular?"

"No, just things in general."

What had once seemed so clear was now muddied. Somehow she had to sort out exactly what she wanted in life—and how much she was willing to risk.

But the days passed, and she found herself no closer to discovering the answers. And if life wasn't complicated enough, her mother seemed determined to make it even more so.

"There is no reason to celebrate my being an old maid," Chas insisted.

Mother waved away her arguments. "My only daughter, my only child, is about to have a birthday, and I plan to celebrate."

"But, Mother," Chas complained, "I'll be twenty-five. Too old to have a birthday party."

"Fine. Then we'll call it something else. How about a celebration of joy?"

Chas shook her head. "I'd just as soon forget the whole business."

"It's important to me," her mother insisted.

Chas studied her mother's face, set in quiet, resolute lines. How could she deny her? Besides, what would be the point? She would find some way of doing what she wanted. "Promise me you won't invite anyone extra, and we'll have just a little celebration with the residents."

Her mother smiled and said, "We'll have a grand time."

Chas turned back to kneading the bread dough, troubled that she had not given her promise.

❧

Chas was almost grateful when the birthday arrived, hoping it would put an end to her mother's furtive whispers behind Chas's back and her hiding things quickly when Chas would enter a room.

Emma baked a big cake and decorated it with icing roses.

"I feel like such a fraud," Chas complained. "All this fuss for nothing."

Emma finished the last rose before she straightened and answered. "It's fun to do something special." She washed the icing from her fingers. "I hope you don't mind, but I invited Gordon."

Chas shrugged. "I don't mind. He'll be the only guest."

Emma gave her a quick look, then busied herself wiping the table. "Your mother is excited about the party."

"All I agreed to was a birthday supper." She studied Emma's bent head. "She didn't do anything I should know about, did she?"

Emma shrugged. "Not that I know of."

Chas waited, suspicion growing in her mind. "I said nothing special."

Emma looked at her, her eyes wide. "I'm sure your mother wouldn't do anything you wouldn't approve of."

"How I wish."

After a quick teatime, Emma ordered Chas out of the house. "You're the birthday girl. I don't want you doing the work, so go away while I finish up meal preparations."

Chas hesitated, but the turkey was cooking in the oven, and the potatoes were peeled. She had gathered lettuce and radishes from the garden earlier. There wasn't a great deal left to do.

"Thank you, Emma. A little time off is the best gift you could give me."

Emma shooed her away.

Chas wandered the streets of the town, enjoying the late summer display of flowers. Already some of the trees looked worn out. The evenings were growing short, the nights cold.

And I'm stuck in a rut.

For weeks she had battled a restlessness she couldn't identify. She had tried to ignore it, explaining it away as missing Colin. Even praying didn't ease it completely. As she walked around town, she determined to use the time alone to sort out her thoughts.

But an hour later she stood in front of the little white house with the picket fence and now-dusty arbor, still searching for answers.

She stared at the house and yard. For so long this little house had symbolized everything she longed for. But now she derived no pleasure from her dreams. What good are empty dreams? she wondered. A little white house with a picket fence meant nothing if she was alone.

Neither the house nor the place provided the security she wanted.

Colin's words rang through her brain.

Love always protects, always perseveres, always trusts, always hopes.

She wanted love.

But she wanted so much more.

She wanted a little house filled with love.

She wanted her mother to be happy and that meant keeping the boardinghouse.

The things she wanted seemed to oppose one another. It was impossible to sort out.

God, please show me what I need to know. Grant me wisdom and patience.

She breathed deeply, letting God's peace fill her, knowing He would lead her to what was best for everyone. After a moment, she turned her steps homeward.

ॐ

The back door opened, and Emma called, "Supper is ready."

"I hope I haven't kept you waiting." Chas couldn't help feeling a little guilty at the amount of time she had spent daydreaming.

"No, Silly. Perfect timing. Come on."

Emma pulled Chas toward the dining room. The first thing Chas noticed was that the connecting door was closed, an unusual occurrence. Then Emma threw open the door and pushed Chas inside.

She gasped. Red, white, and blue streamers hung across the

ceiling to the corners of the room, and bouquets of bright flowers flooded the table.

"Oh, my!" she murmured, blinking.

No extra company, she had insisted. Nothing special. Gordon Simpson she had expected, but not Doc Johnson, Pastor Simpson, and Miss Martha, Michael—and Adam, grinning enough to split his face in two.

ten

"Happy birthday!" everyone shouted.

Chas shot a scolding look at her mother, who only smiled and said, "You're to sit in my place tonight."

Emma pushed her toward the head of the table.

Chas spent several seconds adjusting herself before she looked at the group seated around the extended table.

Mr. Elias beamed at her from the far end.

To her left sat her mother, with Mrs. B at her side.

On Chas's other side, Adam was so close she could say with certainty that he had very recently shaved with a soap reminding her of pine trees after a rain. Michael sat next to him with the others filling in the places on either side.

Michael grinned. "I think we succeeded in surprising you."

"I wasn't expecting this. Mother promised me she wouldn't do anything special."

Mother sighed. "What would be the fun in that? Besides, I never promised."

Adam chuckled. "Your mother has been planning this for weeks."

Chas had promised herself not to look at him until her surprise and confusion had settled. She feared her heart would be in her face, that he would see things she didn't want him to see. But her eyes seemed to have a will of their own and sought him. His blue eyes flashed with laughter, unblinking as they met her gaze.

Her pulse beat wildly behind her temples. She was trapped by his look, floating to the sky.

"It's such fun to surprise you."

Beryl's voice provided escape. Chas tore herself away from the sparkling fire.

"It's so kind of everyone," she murmured.

Emma laughed. "I thought you would come home early and discover us."

Chas grinned. "And here I was feeling guilty about wasting the afternoon."

Mrs. B turned to Mother. "I thought it was meal time."

Everyone laughed, and Emma sprang to her feet. "I'll serve things."

When Chas pushed back to help her, Emma frowned. "You sit. Gordon will help me."

The young man jumped to his feet with an eagerness that made everyone laugh.

After they had filled their plates, Mr. Elias asked Adam, "The delegation from the city has come and gone. Was it a successful visit?"

"Very. Besides making several purchases, they've asked me to set up a display in Calgary. They talked about renting a shop and having a more or less permanent place for my work."

Every word he spoke zinged along Chas's spine. If only she dared love him. If only she could accept the love he had offered her.

Had offered. Past tense. How perverse her nature was that, since he seemed to view her now as nothing more than an acquaintance, she was almost willing to admit she cared about him as more.

"You might be interested in the man who came to the shop today," Adam said.

Grateful to have something to divert her confusing thoughts, Chas forced her attention to his news, reminding herself her feelings could not be allowed to rule her heart.

"He put up a poster advertising hot-air balloon rides."

Everyone talked at once. One by one, Adam sorted out their questions, answering as best he could.

"He'll be in town next week. He's arranged for my father to collect the fee and set up a schedule."

"Time for the cake." Emma and Gordon hurried to the

kitchen, where muffled giggling could be heard.

Emma came back bearing the cake. Gordon's arms were filled with gifts. Everyone sang "Happy Birthday!"

Chas groaned. "I'm too old for a birthday party."

Mother patted her hand. "It's not a birthday party—it's a celebration."

Chas laughed so hard she had to wipe her eyes. "Mother, you are priceless. If this isn't a birthday party, I don't know what is."

Mother had the good grace to look sheepish. "You said no birthday party, so it's not a birthday party."

Everyone laughed. After that it seemed the room rang with laughter.

"Cake or gifts first?" Emma asked.

The guests called out, "Gifts!"

Chas nodded, allowing Gordon to pile them in front of her.

The first was from Mr. Elias, a monogrammed silk handkerchief. "Thank you. It's lovely."

There was a book of poems from Michael, a blouse from Emma, a crocheted doily from Mrs. B, who beamed when Chas thanked her. Knowing the pleasure and pain Mrs. B got from her handwork made the item more precious than she could have imagined.

Beryl and Louise had gone together to buy a lovely box of body powder. Pastor Simpson and Miss Martha gave her a tiny black devotional book.

"Sweets for the sweet," Doc said as Chas unwrapped his gift—a bag of toffees.

Chas giggled. As far back as she could remember, Doc had come on her birthday with the same gift and the same teasing words.

Two gifts remained. She opened the flat one from Adam first. Inside was a miniature painting of Ellen and her the day they had gone to the falls. Tears blurred her vision.

"Thank you," she said softly. She wished she could bring back the day with all its pleasure. It seemed so long ago.

Quieting the trembling of her fingers, she reached for the last package. It was a black lacquered box from John and Roy and the Knutsen boys. When she flipped it open, she gasped. It was filled with money.

It was all she could do not to cry.

"Now my gift," her mother said.

But before she could stand to her feet, Adam jumped up. "I'll get it."

He disappeared into the hall, returning with a large flat package covered in brown paper.

Chas looked from Adam to her mother. "What have you two been up to?"

As he pulled out his chair and propped the present on it, Adam grinned.

Mother fairly bounced in her chair. "Open it. I can't wait to see it."

Everyone laughed.

"I guess this explains all the whispering between the two of you." Chas ripped the protective paper away and gasped.

"It's beautiful!"

An angel, hidden in clouds so that he seemed a part of them, reached down, almost touching a young woman making her way along a winding country road. The young woman was Chas. A brass plaque at the bottom bore the title "Chastity's Angel."

She bent closer. The angel looked exactly like Colin. She glanced up at Adam.

"But you never saw Colin."

"Your guest, Colin?" At her nod he shook his head. "No, he left before I returned from my trip. Why do you ask?"

"Because this angel has his face."

Everyone leaned close to the painting.

"It *is* Colin," Emma murmured, her voice filled with awe. "How did you know how he looked?"

Adam seemed confused. "I never saw him."

"Maybe he was truly an angel," Mother said quietly.

Chas sat back in her chair. Was it possible? Had Colin been an angel? She cherished the thought—her own angel coming with news of a father she had secretly longed for her entire life.

After cake and tea, Michael left. When Chas rose to help with the dishes, Emma chased her from the room.

"You'll not be doing any work this evening."

Emma grinned at Gordon, who rose to his feet and said sheepishly, "I'll give Emma a hand with the dishes."

Beryl and Louise offered as well, but Emma shooed them away. "You let us do them."

"Would you care to sit out on the veranda with me?"

Adam's voice was so close that she felt his breath. She turned to face him, instantly wishing she hadn't. His eyes, the color of rushing water, blazed through her reason. Swallowing hard, she blinked and forced herself to look across the room. She wouldn't let herself be foolish just because the evening had left her unsettled. But she let him lead the way out the back door to the narrow bench where he sat down beside her. Neither of them spoke. Chas listened to the evening sounds—a child calling to another, a dog barking, a bird whistling in a nearby tree. Dusk draped them, soft and gentle.

Finally Chas broke the stillness. "You're sure you've never seen Colin?"

"I suppose I must have seen his face somewhere."

"Do you think it's possible he's an angel?"

Adam shrugged. "Do angels get sick? And why did he come here?"

"I don't know if angels get sick, but can you think of a better way of getting invited into this house?" She rushed on. "He came for a specific reason. You see, he brought Mother and me each a letter from my father."

Adam sat forward, turning to look at her. The light from the window behind them cast golden shadows over his features, drawing them sharply. "Simon LaBlanc? You heard from him after all these years? Where is he?"

She gulped back a sudden rush of tears. "He's dead now," she whispered, pausing. "Colin cared for him at the end. Father wrote the letters before he died."

Adam drew in a sharp breath and sat back.

"Colin says he repented and turned to God before he died." She blinked back tears as she met Adam's eyes. His gaze searched her face and studied her eyes.

"How do you feel about all this?"

She gave a tremulous smile. "Good."

Suddenly she was aware of how good it felt to hear from her father, to know who he was and that he had wished for healing between them. She searched for words to explain it.

"Hearing from him, even though he was already gone, has satisfied something inside me. Like suddenly something that's hurt all my life is healed."

He nodded. "I'm glad."

"Colin told me something else too. He said I should follow my heart."

Adam's look never faltered. "What did he mean?"

She lowered her eyes, needing time to sort out all the things racing through her mind. "I think he saw how I feared so many things. I was afraid I would make a mistake and end up alone. I think not having a father has somehow made me feel I had to build a safe, predictable future for myself."

"And now?" His words were low, insistent.

Chas laughed, tossing her hands in a helpless gesture. "I don't know if I can put it into words, but I feel as if my heart is growing." She shrugged. "I know it doesn't make sense, but that's how I feel."

Adam continued to study her. "Was Michael part of trying to create a safe future?"

She looked at him and nodded, unable to tear her gaze away from his. "I think he was. Poor Michael."

Adam let out his breath sharply. Then his eyes seemed to darken. Or perhaps, Chas reasoned, it was only that the last of the light had faded from the sky.

"And now," he asked, "are you ready to step out of your safe place?"

Chas knew what he meant. His look was intense and probing, his eyes steady and unblinking.

"I'm not sure," she whispered. "Perhaps. I think I'm getting close."

A quick reaction flickered across his face—too fast for Chas to be able to tell what he thought. He stood to his feet and stretched.

"I should be getting home."

He faced her again, his gaze darting to her lips, then resting on her eyes.

"Great birthday party," he murmured. "Happy birthday."

He stepped off the veranda and then turned back to her. "Chas, my feelings haven't changed. I still love you. You will be forever in my heart, but only you will know when you're ready to accept my love."

She nodded, her throat too full for her to speak.

He hesitated and then walked down the path and out of sight.

She waited until her pounding heart had calmed before she hurried to her room.

Her birthday painting stood on the chair. She sat on her bed and studied it. Adam was a wonderful artist. This painting was not only beautiful, but it almost breathed peace and safety.

And he said he still loves me.

She hugged herself even as her mind struggled with the implications. Loving Adam carried with it risks. She had to be very sure she was willing to accept those risks before she allowed herself to love him in return.

Colin seemed to speak to her from the picture. "Follow your heart. Love protects, trusts, perseveres, hopes."

Was she capable of that sort of love? Was her heart strong enough to trust Adam's love even when he felt the need to wander? Was it strong enough to persevere when he took to the roads, to remain behind waiting and patient? Or to leave the security of her home and accompany him? These were questions she must answer. And until she could, reason must prevail.

The next night, sitting on her mother's bed, she asked, "How do I know the right thing to do?"

All day she had thought about the choices she faced and was no closer to knowing what she should do than she had been twenty-four hours earlier.

"What do you desire in your heart of hearts, *ma cherie?*"

Chas picked at a thread on the bedcover. "I love Adam, but I'm afraid of loving unwisely."

Her mother's hands grew still, and for a moment she didn't speak. Chas waited, knowing she was praying and thinking.

"Chastity, never fear love. The love of a good man is a precious gift from God."

"But what if—?" She couldn't bring herself to point out how it hadn't been such a good gift for her mother.

Lifting her hand to still Chas's words, her mother continued slowly. "Adam is a good man. He is nothing like your father was. Nor are you as senseless and headstrong as I was at your age. No, *ma cherie,* you have shown yourself time and again to be wise, steadfast, and strong."

Chas lay back and studied the ceiling. Was she wise, steadfast, and strong? Strong enough to face the challenges a life with Adam would bring?

Later, alone in her room, she paged through her Bible, praying for assurance about her future. She sighed. Life was so uncertain. She couldn't begin to guess what lay ahead. Of course, that was true no matter what choices she made. Or even if she let things continue as they were and refused Adam's love.

An ache grew inside her until the tears sprang to her eyes. Life without Adam was a bleak prospect.

But how could she prove to him—and to herself—that she was willing and capable of stepping outside her safe little world?

And prove it she must. For her own satisfaction. She had to

know she could deal with the challenges Adam's way of life
would surely bring.

❧

The poster hanging in the window of Silverhorn's Mercantile
was large and colorful. Chas stared at it a long time, studying
every detail.

The canopy of the balloon hovered over the basket in which
two people laughed and waved.

It was so unlike her to want to do such a thing.

Always she had done the sensible thing. Suddenly it wasn't
enough. She wanted to fly. Her fingers curled around the wad
of money in her pocket. It was extravagant, but she was sure
the boys would approve, and not stopping to analyze her
motives, she marched to the counter and plunked the money
down in front of Mr. Silverhorn.

❧

The balloon was bigger than she had thought it would be—
and noisier. She listened to the instructions closely, excitement and fear combining to make her mouth dry.

She crawled into the basket. The burners hissed. And then
they slowly lifted from the ground, rising gracefully. Chas
looked down at the tops of trees and houses and the startled,
upturned faces. Not a breath of wind stirred.

The burner puffed out hot air, the sound making her jump.
A bubble of joy filled her heart, bursting forth in a shout of
laughter. She could never have imagined flying was so free-
ing. It was like floating in God's hand.

*"In God have I put my trust. I will not be afraid what man
can do unto me."*

The words swelled within her.

*I will not be afraid of risk or change. I will not fear Adam's
way of life.*

Her heart felt ready to explode into a shower of light over
the side of the basket.

They drifted across the treetops, leaves flashing like golden
coins, over meadows dotted with cows and horses, over gardens

with mounds of potatoes and carrots dug up ready to be put in root cellars, over yellowed stubble and pale stacks of straw that seemed as insignificant as a bubble in the surface of the earth.

The hour was up much too soon. The pilot masterfully brought them safely back to the ground.

Laughing, she let the pilot help her step from the basket. Preparing to take pictures of the balloon ride, Adam stood beside his camera, his jaw slack. He hurried toward her.

"You went up in the balloon?"

She laughed at his expression. "You make it sound as if I walked on water. All I did was go on a little balloon ride."

"Did you think about the risks?"

"It seemed perfectly safe to me." Her smile faltered at the stern look on his face.

"Well, it isn't. How could you do such a silly thing?"

She tried to keep back her laughter and failed. It ended up half guffaw, half giggle. "It was wonderful! I wouldn't have missed it for the world."

He glared at her.

"Now I can understand why you need to experience some things for yourself." She grew thoughtful. "No one could have described this for me."

He adjusted a knob on his camera and fiddled with the black cloth. "Sometimes there's no need for firsthand experience." He shuffled his feet. "We need to talk."

"All right."

"Let me finish here, and then we'll go someplace."

"Sounds good."

He nodded toward a buggy. "Do you mind waiting?"

"Not at all." Welcoming the chance to watch Adam work, she settled on the ground beside the buggy as a couple prepared to enter the basket.

Adam slid in a plate and ducked under the cloth. He took several photos as the balloon filled and rose gracefully.

While he was working, he glanced toward Chas several

times, his expression puzzled.

She hugged her secret to herself.

Finally he folded the tripod and tucked it under his arm.

She jumped to her feet as he headed toward her, an unsteady pulse throbbing along her veins.

"Are you finished?" she asked, although the answer was self-evident.

He shook his head as if to clear it. "For now."

He packed his equipment in the back and helped her to the seat, the buggy dipping as he climbed up beside her.

Without saying anything more, he flicked the reins and headed down the road. Before they reached town, he turned into a side road.

Chas's heart began to dance.

He reined in near a thick stand of trees.

"Shall we walk?"

"I'd like that." He reached up for her, his warm hands lighting fires that sped along her spine to her heart, where they crescendoed into a mighty roar. Although grateful for his hands steadying her, she knew she wouldn't be able to stop quivering until his touch ended.

They fell into step. Chas clenched her hands together. This walk was as daunting as the balloon ride had been, full of promise, yet at the same time fraught with a sense of having lost her moorings. She fortified herself with the reminder of how exhilarating the balloon ride had been.

Adam stopped, turning to look at her.

She lifted her face, letting his gaze search hers until he found what he sought. She knew the moment he did, for his blue eyes glittered with triumph. Her heart swelled against her ribs.

"I can't believe you went on that ride," he murmured.

"I saw the poster and thought, 'I have to fly.' It was as simple as that." His look lifted her heart toward the heavens.

He trailed a finger down her cheek. "Are you really ready to fly?"

She knew he wasn't referring to another balloon ride. "I believe I am," she murmured, her thoughts scattering as she took in the rugged line of his jaw and his golden lashes. The musky scent of his nearness filled her senses until she could think of nothing else.

Slowly he lowered his head, his lips touching hers in the barest hint of a kiss. As he drew back, she strained forward, longing for more.

He gave a low-throated chuckle and pulled her into his arms, taking her lips in a breath-stopping, satisfying kiss that seemed to last forever yet ended far too soon.

She nuzzled her face into his shoulder. She could feel his breath sifting through her hair. She didn't want the embrace to end, but he sighed and lifted her face.

"We need to discuss some things."

She smiled into his eyes.

He lifted her chin. "Are you really ready for this?"

She knew what he meant: Was she ready for the sort of life he offered? But she pretended to misunderstand him and, closing her eyes, tilted her face, offering her lips.

He drew her to him and kissed her again.

Finally he pulled away. "Let's try again," he muttered and, guessing she would again misinterpret his meaning, drew back another inch. "And I don't mean that." His eyes darkened. "We'll save that for later."

She smiled again, relishing the promise. "What did you mean?" she inquired, her voice full of pretended innocence.

He looked beyond her. "I won't make any promises I don't intend to keep. There will be times I go on trips either to show my work or to see something." He looked deep into her eyes. "Though I can't imagine ever wanting to leave you, even for a minute. You'll simply have to come with me."

His confession went straight to the depths of her heart, and she cradled it there, knowing she would forever remember the way he looked at her.

"I promise you this, Chastity LaBlanc—I will love you

forever with all my heart. And if I have to travel for some reason and you can't accompany me, you have my assurance I will hurry home to you as fast as I can."

"Adam Silverhorn, I love you."

Light flooded her gaze until the rest of the world vanished, and she saw nothing else but Adam.

He cupped her face in his hands and kissed her gently and reverently.

"I have dreamed of this for so long," he murmured between kisses. "What made you change your mind?"

"I suppose you could say I grew up." She smiled, thinking of the path her maturing had followed, the role Colin had played. "I've learned security isn't found in a place or a position or even promises. It's found in God and the love He provides. Love protects, perseveres, trusts, hopes."

His expression was hungry, asking for more.

"I understand about your having to travel. I can live with it, knowing you will hurry back. I believe my love is strong enough to accept that. Just as your love was strong enough to wait for me."

Her heart was so full. She had so much she longed to say to him, but she could not find the words. Then his lips found hers again, and she knew sometimes words were unnecessary.

๛

Chas lay on the bed beside her mother, only half listening. Her thoughts lingered on Adam's good-night kiss. They had agreed they would delay their marriage until after Christmas to give them time to sort out the details of their lives. But sometimes it seemed impossible to wait.

"We need to discuss the boardinghouse," Mother said.

Chas gathered up her thoughts. From the day she had told her she and Adam were to marry, her mother had wanted to know their plans regarding the boardinghouse. Chas had been honest. "We haven't planned that far ahead." Now she rolled to her side so she could look into her mother's face.

"I don't want you worrying about it, Mama. Adam and I are

both content to leave things in God's hands."

Mother nodded. "I've come to a decision. I'm going to sell the house."

Chas sat up straight. "Sell?" She gulped. "You always said you wouldn't."

"Doc and I have been talking. He says I might as well accept the facts. Chances are I'll never get well enough to run this place on my own again." She held up a hand. "And I saw when you were thinking of marrying Michael that making the house your responsibility would never allow you to have a normal married life."

"But, Mother, Adam is not Michael. We've discussed it and feel sure things will work out."

Mother smiled serenely. "And they have. Gordon has made me a very pleasant offer." She nodded. "I've accepted it."

Chas fell back on the bed. "Gordon Simpson?"

"He's an astute young man. He'll run the house efficiently, and I've no doubt he'll make a tidy profit."

"Emma?" Was there another wedding in the future? A tiny thought troubled Chas. Would Emma end up being worked to death?

"No one has said anything, but I've got eyes. Emma is very capable, and Gordon has already shown himself to be useful."

Chas relaxed. "You're right. He doesn't seem to mind helping."

He had peeled vegetables, washed lettuce, iced cakes. Until now Chas thought it had been simply a way of spending time with Emma, but now she could see he truly liked the work.

"He's good at fixing things too." He had saved Chas a call to the handyman by repairing the washing machine and fixing the front step. "He's perfect for the job, Mama."

"I thought so myself."

They laughed together, but one thing still troubled Chas.

"What about Mrs. B?"

"Why, that's the best of it. Gordon has made inquiries about a little house for me. He says the Mellon house on the corner is for sale. He's going to make an offer for me. Mrs. B will live with me."

Chas thought of the cozy house, tucked away behind some trees with a front veranda close enough to the street to visit from the front gate. "It's lovely." She sighed. So many changes. All good, but so much to deal with.

"I think it will be good for Mrs. B. I'll have more time to spend with her. Perhaps I can get her to sit outside on the veranda on nice days. She'd enjoy that."

"And it will also make it easier for you to leave the boardinghouse."

Mother took her hand and squeezed it. "I'm looking forward to the move."

Two weeks after she had told Adam her mother's decision, he came to the house to ask Chas if she had time for a walk.

"Go ahead," Emma said. "Gordon and I can manage."

"Thanks." Chas smiled, but Emma had already turned back to Gordon.

The days had been filled with making arrangements for the sale, deciding what to take, what to leave, painting and preparing her mother's house. Through it all, Emma and Gordon had shown themselves more than adequate to run the boardinghouse.

She and Adam sauntered along the streets. Autumn had made her flashiest show and now seemed spent. When Chas would have followed her regular pattern and headed past the big houses to the white picketed yard, Adam turned toward the street paralleling Main Street. Chas was too busy telling of the packing and arranging to give it more than a passing thought.

"I want to show you something." He pulled her to a stop.

"What?" She searched his face for a clue.

"This," he said, pointing. "This house," he added when her expression remained puzzled.

"What about it?"

"I want to buy it, but I want your opinion first."

She lifted her gaze to the house. It was large, two full stories. Her first thought was that it was large enough for boarders. Her spirits dropped.

"I know it's not the little white house with the picket fence, but come inside and let me tell you what I have in mind."

She followed, waiting as he unlocked the door. He closed the door behind her and pulled her into his arms. "I've discovered how much I want to be close to you all the time, so I thought of moving my shop to the front of the house." He trailed kisses along her cheek, sending waves of delight through her. "That way I can slip out and kiss my sweet wife whenever the shop is quiet."

She nestled closer.

"The rest of the house will be ours and ours alone. Except"— he paused to shower more kisses upon her face—"except for the little ones who will fill the rooms."

Tears welled up in the back of her eyes at the thought of little Silverhorns.

"Do I get to see the rest of the house?" she asked him, smiling.

"In a minute." He kissed her soundly.

It took much longer than a minute to see the house with their having to pause for a kiss in each room and to congratulate themselves on how happy they were.

Then he led her to the backyard. She gasped. The yard was so sheltered by trees that it was entirely private. Tucked away in the far corner, surrounded by almost bare bushes, stood a tiny gazebo, still shining with newness.

"It's perfect," she murmured.

He pulled her back into his arms. "My sweet Chas, I will love you forever and do everything in my power to make you happy."

She cradled his face in her hands. "Adam, all I need to make me happy is you."

She kissed him gently and then took his hand and led him

to the gazebo. Under the latticed shadows, the now leafless vines crackling merrily around them, she faced Adam, their intertwined hands pressed to his chest.

"There's something I want to do," she whispered. "Something I promised myself I would do if I ever had a place like this."

He smiled down at her, waiting.

"I want to dedicate this place and our marriage to God. I truly believe He sent Colin to guide me, to show me how to go ahead in my life."

" 'Chastity's Angel.' "

"That painting will always have a prominent place in our home."

"Let's dedicate ourselves and this place to God. I owe Him my deepest thanks for your love." He took her hands, adoring her with his eyes, and then they knelt side by side in the damp leaves.

She closed her eyes as Adam prayed aloud. A whisper of warm breeze swirled around them. She knew it was only the wind, but for a moment she felt as if Colin stood beside them, smiling his approval.

"Thank You, God," she said softly.

A Letter To Our Readers

Dear Reader:

In order that we might better contribute to your reading enjoyment, we would appreciate your taking a few minutes to respond to the following questions. We welcome your comments and read each form and letter we receive. When completed, please return to the following:

Rebecca Germany, Fiction Editor
Heartsong Presents
PO Box 719
Uhrichsville, Ohio 44683

1. Did you enjoy reading *Chastity's Angel* by Linda Ford?
   ☐ Very much! I would like to see more books
      by this author!
   ☐ Moderately. I would have enjoyed it more if

   _____

   _____

   _____

2. Are you a member of **Heartsong Presents**? Yes ☐ No ☐
   If no, where did you purchase this book?_____

   _____

3. How would you rate, on a scale from 1 (poor) to 5 (superior), the cover design?_____

4. On a scale from 1 (poor) to 10 (superior), please rate the following elements.

   _____ Heroine _____ Plot

   _____ Hero _____ Inspirational theme

   _____ Setting _____ Secondary characters

5. These characters were special because_____

_____

_____

6. How has this book inspired your life?_____

_____

_____

7. What settings would you like to see covered in future
   Heartsong Presents books?_____

_____

_____

8. What are some inspirational themes you would like to see
   treated in future books?_____

_____

_____

9. Would you be interested in reading other **Heartsong
   Presents** titles?   Yes ☐   No ☐

10. Please check your age range:
    ☐ Under 18   ☐ 18-24   ☐ 25-34
    ☐ 35-45   ☐ 46-55   ☐ Over 55

Name _____

Occupation _____

Address _____

City _____ State _____ Zip _____

Email _____